The Beasts of Shadow

The Wolf Underneath

N. M. LAMBERT

N. M. LAMBERT

Green Tree Press Edition, 2024

THE WOLF UNDERNEATH

Green Tree Press, LLC
522 N. Central Ave #831 SMB #11019
Phoenix, AZ 85004
www.greentreepublications.org

Published in the United States of America

ISBN: 978-1-963062-00-7

BOOKS BY N. M. LAMBERT

The Threatening Souls series

Threatening Souls

Bleeding Misery

Twisted Ignorance

Immortal Injustice

The Days of Darkness series

Days of Darkness

The Beasts of Shadow trilogy

The Wolf Underneath

To anyone who ever felt different or like they didn't belong, this one's for you.

A NOTE FROM THE AUTHOR

This book is very different from my previous books. It is lighter than my other ones, but it still deals very heavily with the topic of grief. Though there are happier moments, the overarching theme of grief is still very present. There is also gore in this story, though it is very minor, as well as anxiety and panic attacks and a brief mention of twin loss. If you prefer happier stories, I understand, but if you're still here despite knowing this, then I'm excited to share with you the beginning of Savannah and Callum's story.

PROLOGUE

SAVANNAH

When I was six, I saw my first dead body.

The alarm sounded in our small village of Ebonrowe, like it did every day after the full moon. I didn't realize what the alarm meant at the time, but my parents always told my brother and I it was something bad and to stay indoors.

I was the oldest, so it was always my job to make sure my brother and I stayed put. But I was also a curious person who craved adventure, and rules were never my strong suit.

So, as soon as my parents left, I buttoned up my wool coat and laced up my leather boots before stomping towards the front door of our small, two-story cabin.

I barely made it to the front door when I heard shuffling behind me. Tentatively, I turned around, and there was my brother, Mathias, staring at me with wide, fearful eyes. His skin was too pale, like he had seen a ghost. And perhaps in that moment, he did as I was about to break the biggest rule in our household.

"Where are you going?" he asked curiously, in the way four-year-olds often did.

"Out," I replied. My answer was clipped and short, devoid of the usual warmth I held when talking to him. Mathias and I weren't like typical siblings. We rarely bickered and did everything together. Because of our parents' coal mining occupations, we were considered outcasts by the other kids in the village, so we had to become our own best friends.

But this was something I had to do alone. I knew I would never hear the end of it if I somehow got my brother killed with my recklessness, and I would never forgive myself if something happened to him. So, I had to be cold in order to protect him as much as myself.

"But Mommy and Daddy said—"

"I won't be gone long," I said as my expression softened. It was the truth, something that would only take mere seconds. I would slip out, see what all the commotion was about, and then slip back in before anyone was the wiser.

Except my brother would know, and I would essentially be asking him to lie to Mom and Dad.

"You won't tell," I said quietly, "will you?"

There was a pause, and I could see the gears turning in Mathias's head. He hated doing anything wrong, which admittedly had gotten him into more trouble than I'd like to admit with the other village kids. A goody-two-shoes, they'd call him. If it wasn't for me ready to whip their asses if any of them laid a hand on Mathias, I was sure he would be the subject of regular beatings.

After what felt like minutes on end, Mathias shook his head, and I exhaled the breath I didn't realize I was holding. He wouldn't tell. I knew this would kill him in the long run, but I was grateful for his silence.

"I'll give you an extra big slice of chocolate cake for dessert today," I promised him, which seemed to light up his features. And then, I was gone, snow crunching beneath my boots as I made my way to the village square.

The shops I passed remained closed, curtains carefully drawn over the windows. And there was absolutely no one out and about, as if I were walking through some sort of ghost town. Such a sight should've unnerved me, but it only piqued my curiosity even more. It was a mystery I had yet to solve, an enigma I needed to conquer.

And then, I finally stumbled upon the village square, and why there was a lack-of people started to make sense. It seemed the entire village, minus the children, were huddled together in a circle, surrounding something I couldn't make out. I dared to creep as close as I could without alerting anyone, using one of the nearby shops as a cover.

As if by some miracle, the people nearest to me parted, and that was when I finally saw what had everyone up in knots. There was a body on the ground with skin as pale as the snow. Deep slashes marred the flesh, dried blood caked over the wounds. And where the stomach should've been, there was a messily cut hole, as if whoever did this dug into the body as if they were just digging through dirt. Intestines spilled out of the gaping hole, mixing with the blood that pooled on the ground.

But the scariest part wasn't what I saw but the fact I knew the person. It was Mrs. Harlow, the village baker, who just yesterday blessed my family with a fresh, steaming loaf of white bread and a tall, decadent chocolate cake, the same one I promised extra to my brother. And now, she was dead as the rest of the village crowded around her.

I wanted to throw up, and so, I did as silently as I could. Now, it was beginning to make sense why my parents were so adamant we didn't leave the house when the alarm went off.

This was something no one should see, let alone a child who had an imagination the size of the entire universe.

But I couldn't unsee it now, and so, I straightened my back and wiped my mouth with the back of my sleeve as I listened to the conversations going on around me.

"It was the beast," a man off to my left said to his wife. "It struck again."

"What do you mean?" his wife, who was trembling beside him, asked.

The man gave an exasperated sigh, as if his wife should already know the answer. "The one that kills every full moon."

Chills skirted down my spine right when another conversation to my right caught my interest.

"Oh god, oh god, oh god!" a girl who looked no older than sixteen wailed as she sobbed into her friend's shoulder.

"It's okay," her friend said, lightly patting her back. "The beast is gone now."

The girl soon shot up as anger burst forth. "Until the next full moon!" she spat. "It'll be okay once we're all dead!"

I backed away slowly, my curiosity now long gone, replaced by fear. Words played over and over again in my mind. *Beast. Full moon. Death.* With the way they were talking, I was sure some sort of animal did this, but as to whether or not the animal was ordinary, I wasn't so sure.

I ran home as fast as my legs could go and flung open the door. My parents weren't back yet, which I took as a good sign, and my brother gazed at me curiously.

"What was it?"

And because no six-year-old should've witnessed that, let alone her four-year-old brother, I lied and said, "Someone stole something from Mrs. Harlow."

In a sense, that was the truth. Something *had* been stolen from Mrs. Harlow, but it wasn't a material good.

Mathias nodded, accepting my answer as truth, and we went upstairs to play with some of my dolls. Neither of us spoke further about the incident.

Every month after that up until I was twelve, I had to pretend I didn't know why the alarms rang the morning after a full moon or why people kept disappearing. That was when my parents sat me down and told me our village was cursed, that a beast shrouded in night killed every full moon. They made me promise not to tell Mathias, that they would tell him themselves in a couple years, when they deemed he was ready for the truth.

Mathias never made it to his twelfth birthday. The night before, a night that so happened to also be a full moon, he snuck out to meet with some buddies he made within the past year for a pre-birthday celebration. He never made it back home.

Instead, my parents and I were met with his lifeless corpse in the center of the village square, along with the bodies of his buddies.

I became the Huntress a month after my brother's death, at the ripe age of fourteen, making it my personal mission to hunt the beast that ripped my best friend away from me. I grew colder and more distant from my parents and anyone else who tried to talk to me, only speaking in clipped, one-word phrases. Everyone thought the trauma of losing my brother was too much for someone as young as me to handle, and perhaps, they were right. The trauma *was* too great, saturating my heart with endless anger.

I took up archery and let everyone believe it was a hobby to help me cope with my trauma. During the day, I would practice, but during the night, I would explore the woods that surrounded our village, hoping to catch the beast unaware.

Hunting the beast was the only thing that gave me purpose. Perhaps if I finally brought down the thing that had been terrorizing my village since before I was born, I could finally mourn my brother properly.

But I never saw the beast, not even on the night of a full moon, as if it were somehow evading me. Meanwhile, more innocent people were dying, and I felt powerless to stop it.

But I refused to give up, and so, I would strap my bow to my waist and a plethora of arrows to my back and continue the journey I had laid out for myself.

ONE

SAVANNAH

I hated birthdays, and my eighteenth one was no different. It was just another painful reminder of something Mathias would never get to experience again.

"Surprise!" my mother and father both yelled as a colossal vanilla cake was set down in front of me. White frosting covered the surface of the cake as strawberries lined the top. In blue cursive were the words, "HAPPY BIRTHDAY, SAVANNAH".

My stomach churned, but I plastered on a fake smile and blew out the candles. I stopped believing in wishes when they never came true, but in that moment, I found myself wishing for the beast to hand themselves to me on a silver platter.

I was the only child my parents had left, so everything they did for me had to be some huge spectacle. Holidays, birthdays, it didn't matter—I was showered with gifts and affection, as if they were afraid I would be ripped away from them too. And I couldn't bring myself to tell them I didn't need all this. What I really needed was my brother.

My father started slicing the cake into thick, even slices and distributed them onto three plates. Three scoops of vanilla ice cream accompanied the slices before the plates were passed out to each of us.

"Are you ready for tomorrow?" my mother asked me as she sat down to enjoy her dessert.

I shoved a piece of cake into my mouth and nodded. I didn't just take up archery in order to slay the beast. It was also something safe I could do that no one would question. Archery was a big deal in my village, the sport everyone seemed the most excited for, and every year, there was an annual archery competition. This year was the first year I was actually eligible to compete, and I was one of twenty people competing for the grand cash prize.

I was excited, but I was also extremely nervous.

"I hear the butcher's daughter, Matilda Brant, is bragging to everyone how she's the best and is going to win," my father said before flashing me a smile. "She has nothing on you, kiddo."

I bristled. Matilda Brant was only a year older than me, and she was perhaps the brattiest person I had ever known. Not a day went by where she wouldn't gallivant around town as if she owned the place with her posse of bitches, barely giving anyone else the time of day. There was once a time where she would shower me with fake sympathy shortly after my brother died, but I always shot her down.

Now, she doesn't like me as much as I don't like her, which doesn't bother me in the slightest. That bitch can shove her ego where the sun doesn't shine.

"Isn't Trevor Browning also competing this year?" my mother asked.

I flinched at the mention of my ex's name. Trevor and I briefly dated last year, and since neither of us knew what we were doing, it was really awkward. We broke up after about two months, and even though it was mutual, the two of us have avoided each other ever since.

"Mom!" I groaned as embarrassment coated my features. Honestly, I didn't know what past me saw in him. All I remembered from that relationship was how bad of a kisser he was.

Slob. Everywhere.

"Sorry, honey!" my mother said apologetically before returning to her cake. But the small smile she gave told me she wasn't sorry at all. She had always liked Trevor and was sad when we broke up. Since then, she always tried to find reasons to bring him up in front of me, as if just by her mentioning his name would cause us to magically get back together.

Fat chance, Mom.

My parents both started talking about something else that I wasn't really paying attention to. I shoveled my dessert into my mouth as quickly as possible before shoving myself up from the table. "Can I be excused?"

My parents blinked at me in surprise. "But we haven't even opened presents yet," my mom said.

"Later, Mom. I'm really tired," I said with a yawn, stretching for good measure.

"Let her go," my dad said, waving me off. "Kid has a big day tomorrow."

I'm not a kid! I wanted to scream but bit my tongue instead. I hadn't felt like a kid in years, not since my brother's death. "Thanks, Dad," I said again, giving him a hug. "And thank you both for the cake. I'll open presents tomorrow. I promise."

And then, I was out of there as fast as I could. I had another hunt scheduled for tonight, and I needed all the rest I could get in the few hours of daylight left.

Sleep came easily to me the moment my head hit my pillow, and my mind gave way to the endless nightmares that had plagued me since my brother's death. They were all the same, my eleven-year-old brother fruitlessly fighting against what my mind presumed was the beast while I helplessly watched behind an impenetrable sheet of glass. Night after night, I would watch his death over and over again until I woke up screaming, drenched in sweat.

When the nightmares first began, my parents would come running whenever they would hear me scream. My mother would hold me as I sobbed while my father went into the kitchen to grab me a warm glass of milk. Now, however, my nightmares have become so commonplace that my parents became immune to the noise of my screams. It was better this way anyway. They already do so much for me, too much at times, that I would just feel more guilty every time they came running at the sound of my demons.

My brother would've been sixteen now, and I think that was the part that tortured me the most. I should've prevented him from going out that night. After all, we both knew the risks. But instead, I sat back and told him to have fun on his birthday eve.

I told him to have *fun*.

Fun was a luxury no one in my family could afford to have ever again, least of all me. Not while the beast that killed my brother was still out there.

After my heart calmed down from watching my brother's death for what seemed like the millionth time, I rolled onto my side towards my window. A blanket of stars filled the night sky, accompanied by the bright, shining moon. It was a waxing gibbous tonight. In just a few short days, the moon would be full again, and the beast would return.

I had to make sure it was dead before that happened.

I shot out of bed and immediately pulled on my boots and slid on my coat. The house was dark and quiet, suggesting my parents had gone to bed, which made it easier for me to sneak out. No one knew I slept at most five hours each night and then went out to hunt until sunrise.

After grabbing my bow and some arrows, I headed out of the house.

The air was cold and brisk, slapping me against my face, my boots loudly stomping against the dirt as I ran towards the forest. The trees swallowed me up, enveloping me in a blanket of darkness as I scanned through the trunks for any sudden movement.

The rustle of bushes to my left snapped my head in that direction, and I narrowed my eyes at what was presumably a rabbit or even a squirrel. A creature so small, it couldn't possibly have caused the amount of damage there was to my brother's body. And sure enough, a plump, brown rabbit, skirted out of the bushes, weaving between the trees and darting into the darkness until it was completely out of sight.

I let out a sigh. Occasionally on the nights of the full moon, I would see random animal carcasses strewn about despite not seeing or hearing the beast myself. It was as if it knew I was looking for it and therefore avoided me.

As if it were scared of my meager bow and arrows.

The thought sent a smile to my lips, and a chuckle burst forth, enveloping me in a sense of familiarity. I used to be so happy. I used to laugh and joke and live in a carefree world with my brother by my side.

And then, I was reminded of why I couldn't laugh, that

I shouldn't be happy, not when my brother's body was buried beneath mounds of dirt.

My hands shook, and I exhaled a breath of sorrow. He should've been here, celebrating my eighteenth birthday with me. I finally crossed the threshold into adulthood, a momentous occasion, and he wasn't here with me.

It seemed with each passing day he wasn't here, my heart shriveled up just a little bit more.

Kill the beast first, I reminded myself, snapping myself out of my depressing thoughts. *Mourn later.* Because I hadn't properly mourned him the way a big sister should, and I couldn't until his killer was dead and gone.

I liked to think my brother would've been proud of me, would've been proud of the young woman I've become on the surface. I knew my parents were proud. They didn't waste time in telling me whenever they could.

But no one knew the darkness that lurked beneath the surface of my skin. And no one *would* know, not until I brought forth the beast's carcass, assuring everyone's safety.

As if on cue, there was a howl in the distance. *Wolf*, I thought, turning my head in the direction of the sound. The pounding of paws soon accosted my ears, sending my heart on overdrive as adrenaline flooded my veins. It sounded like a wolf, but at the same time, it didn't. Deeper. Richer.

And the paws were like giants, thumping across the forest floor without a care in the world.

A single word filtered through my subconscious. *Beast.*

It vibrated my body in endless adrenaline, a Huntress on the war path to incapacitate her prey.

Beast. Beast. Beast.

I took off through the forest, following the pounding of paws. My lungs screamed as I pushed them harder than I ever have before, the brisk night air washing over my face.

The beast was close. I knew it in my gut.

There was another howl, sending my heart even more on overdrive. The grip on my bow tightened in anticipation.

Tonight was the night it would finally end. Tonight, I would finally lay my demons to rest and carry on with my life, honoring my brother's memory with everything I had.

Tonight was the night the beast would finally go down, its body burning in the middle of the village square for all to see.

The thought spurred me on, and I ran harder than I've ever run before. *Beast, beast, beast,* my mind continuously chanted.

I broke through a piece of thicket, feeling the thorns scratch my skin through my clothes. But I barely felt the pain, for directly in front of me was the biggest and most beautiful white wolf with the most piercing blue eyes I had ever seen. And it wasn't alone.

Accompanying the white wolf was an equally magnificent brown one with eyes the color of rich chocolate. The two of them were scurrying through the forest, nipping at each other's heels as they ran.

If it weren't for my mission, I would've watched as they

played, enamored by their size and beauty. But even I knew the most beautiful things were always the most deadly, and so, I drew my bow and nocked my first arrow.

In all my thoughts, I never considered the possibility of there being *two* beasts. It was a scary and sobering thought as I aimed my arrow at the white wolf, fingers poised to let it launch.

Better safe than sorry, I thought. And then, I let my arrow fly.

The wolves suddenly took off before my arrow made contact, and instead of burrowing into the meat of the stomach, my arrow lodged itself into the white beast's shoulder. The worst cry of pain I had ever heard pierced the quiet night air, and I fought the urge to cover my ears.

The brown beast ran off, disappearing further into the forest, while the white one fell behind a peculiar set of rose bushes.

The brown one got away, but it didn't matter because the white one was still within my grasp.

I would just have to come back another night for the one that got away.

I sprinted to the bushes, another arrow nocked and ready to fly.

Yet as I peered into the bushes, I wasn't met with the magnificent form of a white wolf.

Instead, what met me was a very unconscious, and very *naked,* boy around my age with pale, porcelain skin and short, cropped hair the color of snow.

And with a very sizeable arrow protruding from his shoulder.

Son of a bitch!

All thought left me as I put my bow aside and crouched next to the boy, feeling the underside of his chin for a pulse. It was still there, beating a sad tune against his skin. But the arrow had shot clean through his shoulder, blood spurting from the wound like an active volcano.

I wasn't a killer. I didn't *kill* people.

"Okay, this is going to hurt like a bitch," I said to no one in particular, taking off my jacket to use as a makeshift bandage as I removed the arrow. A wet popping sound followed, the arrow coated in the boy's blood as it slid easily out of the wound.

I tossed the arrow aside, pressing the jacket against the wound to keep more blood from spilling out. Because damn it if I let an innocent boy die because of my revenge mission.

Fucking hell!

I couldn't leave this boy out here alone with a gaping wound I had caused. My morals wouldn't allow it. But there was nowhere I could take him without raising suspicions. Nowhere except…

A thought suddenly came to me, albeit probably one of the stupidest thoughts I had ever had. Without giving me a chance to think it through, I returned my bow to my back and reached under the boy's armpits, securing him in a hold and trying not to jostle his wound too much as I dragged him through the forest back to my house.

Back to my attic, where no one went anymore. A journey that took hours upon hours.

I didn't know how I managed to do so with minimal blood spilling out, but soon, he was holed up in my attic with a blanket around his naked form and a fresh bandage covering both sides of the wound.

And throughout the entire endeavor, the boy hadn't woken up once.

TWO

CALLUM

There were days where I wished I could strangle my wolf. Today was one of those days.

"Come on!" I huffed to myself, my muscles straining, as I fought to lift the last of what felt like a hundred-pound rock onto the wooden platform next to me. Nine more rocks of the same size already littered the platform, forming an open circle with one more space remaining for the tenth rock.

Nine rocks I had already lifted and placed, about to be joined by the tenth one. And my wolf wasn't cooperating, lending me some of his strength so I could complete the task and be done with it.

Instead, my wolf sequestered himself deep within my subconscious, adamantly *not* listening to my cries for help.

Stupid fucking alpha—

"Callum!" my father boomed, the sound of his voice causing me to fumble, and the rock I was trying so hard to lift came crashing down mere inches from the platform.

Damn it! I huffed, straightening my back, as I turned to meet the judgmental stare of my father. Judgmental, because I had yet again failed another one of his test.

Today was such a simple strength test that should've been a breeze with my wolf. Move all the rocks to the platform in ten minutes or less. Five or less meant I passed with flying colors. Seven or less meant I passed, but there were still areas I could improve upon. Ten or less meant I passed, albeit begrudgingly.

Any more than ten meant I was an automatic failure, another reason for me *not* to become the future alpha of my pack. But as an only child, I was the only option, and as such, I couldn't afford to fail.

Failure meant leaving my pack without a successor in case something were to happen to my father. It meant another family could swoop in and take our place.

My father's position as alpha in our secluded wolf pack had always been secure until I came along. At only five years old, he had mastered complete control over his wolf, and at ten, he had mastered all his training and tests.

I, on the other hand, hadn't mastered anything, least of all my wolf, even though I was the ripe age of nineteen. An embarrassment, by pack standards, seeming to not have inherited any of my father's gifts.

"You failed," came my father's booming voice, yanking me out of my thoughts. "Yet again. Have you learned nothing?"

I shriveled underneath my father's glare. He was a true alpha, able to dominate with nothing more than a glance. Whereas I, on the other hand, was a sorry excuse for an heir, seeming to only be that in name only.

"Go easy on him!" my mother begged, coming to my father's side and laying a comforting hand on his arm. "The boy tried his best!"

My father grunted. "Margaret," he warned before shaking his head. "His best isn't good enough. How will he ever garner enough respect from the pack to become the next alpha if he keeps failing?"

"I didn't master my wolf until I was twenty!"

"You are also not next in line to become the alpha!" my father snapped, causing my mother to wince in surprise. His facial features softened. "Margaret, I...I'm sorry."

"No," my mother hissed. "I heard you loud and clear, *Xander*! You don't think we're good enough!"

My father bristled. "That's not what I meant, and you know it. Of course you're good enough. You're *more* than good enough."

"But our son isn't?"

My father breathed deeply. In and out. In and out. "As my future successor, there are different standards for him than there are for you. The pack won't accept a weak alpha!"

I knew what was coming before I heard the smack as my mother's hand made contact with my father's cheek. The skin swelled an angry red as nothing but shock was plastered on my father's face. Then, my mother spun around and headed for the house, yelling, "You're sleeping outside tonight!"

My father stared at her retreating form, dumbfounded. "What'd I do?"

For someone as dominant as my dad, he was absolutely clueless when it came to matters of the heart. "You just called her weak, Dad," I said, coming to his side.

"I didn't…" My dad sighed, finally turning to face me. "All I said was—"

"The pack won't accept a weak alpha, ergo I'm weak," I said nonchalantly. "And she took that to mean *she's* weak as well."

My dad shook his head, bewildered. "She's a submissive. You're *supposed* to be a dominant. That's not even close to being the same thing!"

I couldn't stop the smile from gracing my lips. "You know, for a pack alpha, you're really clueless when it comes to women."

At this, my father belted out a laugh. "That may be true." He paused, the smile fading from his lips. "Just so you know, I don't think you're weak. But I *do* think you're behind, and…" He sucked in a deep breath. "I worry for you, Callum. Now more than ever, the pack needs a strong alpha, and I worry what will happen if you get rejected by Alonsia."

This time, it was my turn to sigh. "If she deems me unworthy, then I'll take whatever consequences she deems appropriate." Alonsia was our goddess, sister to the witch goddess, Hectora, and the supposed mother of all wolf shifters on the planet. Without her, we wouldn't exist, and as such, we let her choose who will lead us. We let her choose whether to approve or reject our selection.

I've only heard stories of what happened to wolves who were rejected by Alonsia. At best, they were executed, but at worst, they faced banishment, cursed to live the rest of their lives without a pack to call home.

Wolves are pack animals. Without a pack to call our own, our minds slowly ebb away until there is nothing left but something feral and unrecognizable. Many of us would consider that a fate worse than death.

I was determined to not let it come to that. My parents would be devastated about my death, sure, but my banishment would destroy them.

"Perhaps I'm just a late-bloomer," I said, trying to lighten the mood.

"Let's hope so," my father said. "Only two months remain until Alonsia makes her decision."

Two months until the blood moon, a time once in a generation when magic was at its strongest. It was then when Alonsia came to us to make her decision.

A decision that would either make or break me.

~*~

My father had no more tests planned for the rest of the day, so I was free to do whatever I wished. Not that it mattered much, since most of my free time was spent conversing with those I would someday lead. As the next alpha, it was my job to get to know every single member of our small pack, listening to their stories and pretending that every word that came out of their mouths was the most interesting thing I've ever heard.

I was never one for small talk, but then again, I wasn't a big socialite either. There was only one person in the entire pack I truly called a friend, and it was because he, like myself, would rather swallow an entire container of bleach than be in the presence of people twenty-four-seven.

Luckily for him, he had a choice. I, however, did not.

When dinner rolled around later that evening, I sat down with the rest of my pack by the roaring fire, watching as the beef we were to consume sizzled above the flames. Wolf shifters were a strange breed, gifted with both wolf and human biology and tendencies. Though we could consume raw meat and not get sick, most of us hated the taste. There were only a few that didn't care either way, and so, we found ourselves always cooking our meat the way full humans did.

I was one of the weird ones who didn't care one way or another, and my father was the same way. He always told me that as alphas, we had to be stronger than anyone else, and apparently, that also included a tolerance for raw meat.

The sound of footsteps pattered to my right, and when I turned my head, I caught the gaze of my best friend, Sammy Bronwen. He was medium-set with dark brown skin and a deep set of brown eyes, his curly, black hair barely sweeping the base of his neck. He took his usual seat beside me, shooting me a quick smile in return.

"How was alpha training today?" he asked almost mockingly, his grin turning sadistic.

I gave him a light shrug, a scowl on my face. "You know how it is."

"Do I?" he raised an eyebrow. "What'd your dad make you do today?"

"Lift rocks," I deadpanned.

"That sounds awful."

"Tell me about it."

The two of us soon fell into a comfortable, introverted silence as we returned our attentions to the fire. My mouth started watering as I breathed in the rich scent of our dinner. There were few things I loved more than a juicy, well-cooked steak.

"How'd you do?" Sammy suddenly asked, his gaze still locked on the fire.

"Hmm?" I hummed.

"Lifting rocks, I mean," Sammy clarified. "How'd you do?"

I gave a nervous snort. "I failed. Again."

If Sammy had been anybody else, I would've expected to be showered with fake sympathy and promises that I would do better next time. Thankfully, however, Sammy wasn't *just* anybody, choosing instead to let the subject drop. "Do you want to go for a run after this?"

"It's late," I said. A blanket of darkness had already descended upon our settlement, the moon clearly shining overhead. And I had to be up early again tomorrow for another one of my father's tests.

"It's not even midnight yet!" Sammy barked. "Please?"

"No, but it's getting close." I sighed. When I was younger, I used to love our late-night runs, but that was before my father started cracking down on my training.

"Just a quick one, Callum," Sammy pleaded, eyes narrowing. "It would probably do you some good."

With shoulders suddenly sagging, I relented. "Okay," I said. "But only half an hour. Anything longer, and I'll scream."

Sammy grinned like he just won a contest. "Deal!"

The meal was served shortly after, and the two of us ate in silence, enjoying each other's company and the crackling of the roaring fire. The beef tasted just as good as it smelled, nearly melting in my mouth with every bite.

When we were done, Sammy led me to the edge of our settlement, bare feet crunching the grass with every step. It'd been a long time since we went on one of our runs, and a pang struck my heart with how much I missed them. How much I missed us as carefree children, before the burden of alphahood wrenched me away.

Sammy was the first to shift as he placed himself directly in front of me. What soon followed was the cracking of bones as brown fur shredded through skin, his limbs growing thick and transforming into a set of four girthy paws that thundered on the ground with each step.

He blinked at me through his wolf's eyes, slow, waiting. And then, he tipped his head up and let the loudest howl I had ever heard rip from his throat.

I smiled. It felt good to spend time with Sammy in this way, like we used to as children. And then, I shifted too, feeling my bones pop as they lengthened and contorted into my own impressive wolf form.

I may have still had trouble controlling my wolf when I was in my human form, but I had no problem shifting on command and letting my wolf take over, at least for a little bit. And it felt good—*natural*—to be on all fours, letting the cool night breeze kiss my white fur as I stood straight, meeting Sammy's gaze.

He bowed his head, a show of submissiveness in the presence of his future alpha. And then, without another word, he took off into the forest.

I sprinted after him as fast as my legs would take me, tongue hanging out as I nipped at his heels. It was always a game for us as we took turns chasing each other, trying to catch the other one. And sometimes, we would race each other through the forest, seeing who was the fastest.

Sometimes I won, and sometimes Sammy won, but it

didn't matter because as long as we were together, everything would be alright.

I nipped at his heels once more as we stumbled into a clearing, stopping for all of two seconds before taking off again. *I've got you now!*

Fat chance! Sammy yelled down our mental link, what allowed us to communicate in our wolf forms. A playful snarl ripped up my throat in response as I got ready to pounce.

A thorn soon pierced my shoulder, causing a howl to rip through my throat. *No, not a thorn,* I corrected.

An arrow. Cleaving all the way through my shoulder.

Callum! Sammy yelled, swiftly turning around. *Hold on! I'm coming!*

No! I ordered through the pain, oozing as much future alpha power as I could through the link. *Go back to the pack! Warn them of what happened and get help!*

Sammy whimpered as he tried to fight against my command, not wanting to leave me. But even now, he couldn't refuse a direct order.

And I was giving him a direct order. To leave me behind while he went to warn the rest of the pack of a potential predator.

Sammy then took off running deeper into the forest, back the way we came.

And I swayed on my feet, black spots dancing across my vision as my back hit the ground hard.

I barely felt my body twisting and contorting back into

my human form before the darkness finally took hold, drowning me in its misery.

THREE

SAVANNAH

I spent the night in the attic, watching over the boy and just hoping, *praying* to any god or goddess who was listening, that he would be okay. That he would wake up, and we would share a laugh, and all would be right in the world.

Yet all night, he never woke up once.

At some point, I must've fallen asleep, for the next thing I knew, sunlight was streaming through the attic windows, illuminating the small space in its golden rays.

I stole a glance at the boy, disappointment panging in my gut when I realized he hadn't moved an inch from when

I left him. My heart sank, and if I didn't know any better, I would've thought he was just slumbering peacefully.

But then, my eyes landed on the blood-soaked bandage, and suddenly, the boy didn't look so peaceful anymore.

I wanted to scream. I wanted to cry. But most importantly, I wanted to know how I managed to screw up as badly as I did. I was *so sure* I had shot the beast. In fact, I remembered watching the arrow pierce its shoulder. I remembered seeing two beasts, but I *didn't* remember seeing another human in sight.

Yet when I went over to finish the job, I was met with a very *naked* boy instead who had taken the arrow meant for the beast.

It didn't make any sense.

I sighed, shifting my position on the floor. I knew basic first aid, but nothing too advanced. Our village infirmary was the one who took care of more serious ailments, but I couldn't possibly bring the boy over to it in the dead of night. It would've led to too many questions I wouldn't have been able to answer.

No, my rudimentary healing skills would have to do, at least for the time being.

My archery competition was an hour or so after lunch, so I still had a fair bit of time until then. As I shifted closer to the boy, I reached out and brushed my fingers over the bandage. I should change it, swap it out for a clean one. I *knew* I should, and yet—

I peeled the bandage back, a gasp lodging in my throat.

Where a still-gaping wound *should've* been, there was now light pink skin fading into the boy's milky white complexion. Not even a scar remained, which nearly sent my head spinning.

Impossible!

There was no way any wound, but especially one of that magnitude, should've healed as quickly as it did. My heart was on overdrive, hands clammy with nervous sweat, as I stared at the space where a wound had been not even twenty-four hours ago.

I blinked, sure my mind was playing tricks on me, but no. The skin remained, no sign of a wound in sight.

I tossed the bandage aside and stumbled backwards, nearly tripping on my boots as I did so. Something wasn't right about the boy, and now that I thought about it, there was no way I missed my mark, not when I *saw* it go into the beast's shoulder.

The only explanation I could come up with was the boy somehow *was* the beast. And if that were the truth, then I just brought a murderer into my home.

During the next hour, I scrambled to secure the boy as quickly as I could, dressing him in some old clothes I knew my dad wouldn't miss, tying his hands and legs together with a couple pieces of thick rope, and securing a leash around his throat that I also tied to a wooden peg over by one of the windows.

Satisfied, I scrambled back to admire my handiwork, preying once again that my bindings would hold. If this boy truly *was* the beast, he would no doubt be very angry when he finally awoke. And if not…

Well, he would still be angry, but hopefully to a lesser degree.

Shaking my head, I proceeded to exit the attic, only sparing one more backwards glance to make sure my bindings still held.

They would have to be enough. Because if they weren't, I may have just doomed my entire town.

~*~

Matilda Brant was still the same snot-nosed brat I came to loathe, strutting around with her bow and arrows strapped pretentiously to her back. I had no doubt her parents bought her a new bow specifically for this competition. They were one of the few families in Ebonrowe who actually had money, and it showed in the way their only daughter dressed and acted. Like she was better than everyone else.

Like she was better than *me*, even though *I* was the one who braved the woods every single night, looking for our village's curse.

"Savannah!" she said cheerily, a huge fake grin plastered on her face. She glided towards me like the princess she pretended to be, two of her bitches in tow. "Fancy seeing you here!"

"You knew I'd be here," I said coldly. It was no secret

this was my first year participating in the archery competition. You had to be at least eighteen, and your first time was *always* a big deal.

Matilda tapped a plump finger against her glossed lips. "Right! Of course! First time and all that," she said, motioning one of her bitches forward. "It's Ronna's first time too!"

The girl who must've been Ronna shuddered, evidently not accustomed to being in the spotlight. Seeming to sense her discomfort, Matilda swiftly elbowed her in the gut, causing her to straighten her posture and tentatively meet my eyes, a puppet told to act intimidating.

But I saw right through her. She didn't truly want to be here, in an environment such as this. She was mousy, the epidemy of the kinds of girls Matilda inducted into her circle. Easy to mold, typical "yes" girls that do what she says without question.

She tells them what they can and can't do, shaping them into the bitches from Hell I've come to know. But she not once tried to do so to me.

I cocked an eyebrow at her, unamused. "And your other puppet?"

If Matilda was offended by my use of the word "puppet", she didn't show it. "Oh, this is just Briana," she said, arching her thumb over her shoulder to where the last girl stood. "She's not competing. Archery isn't really her thing."

"Of course," I said, fighting the urge to shake my head.

Then, I plastered on a fake smile, feeling my cheeks burn from the sudden strain. "Well, may the best archer win."

And then, before Matilda could utter another word, I turned my back on them. Purposely. I had no patience for bullies, and Matilda was the worst of them all.

The archery competition took place in the center of the town square. Every year, surrounding businesses were closed, and stands of every food and beverage imaginable populated the outer skirts of the square. On the surrounding buildings themselves were various archery targets, all positioned at various points of height and accessibility.

Directly in the center was an elongated table complete with extra bows and arrows, in case we couldn't or didn't want to bring our own. There was also a single white marking a few inches in front of the table, made in tape, where we were to stand as we shot at the various targets.

The spectacle never ceased to amaze me. Even before my brother's death, I remembered attending every single year, always amazed by each's archer's grace and accuracy. Now, it was finally my turn to *be* one of those graceful archers, and to say I was nervous would've been an understatement.

I was so lost in thought, I didn't see the wall directly in front of me until I ran into it. *No, not a wall,* I corrected as I stumbled backwards, nearly tripping over my feet. *A person.* And not just any person.

Trevor Browning. The one person, besides Matilda, I

had no desire to see, though for a different reason. Things were still really awkward between us.

There was a reason we avoided each other like the plague.

There was no avoiding each other now, however, not when we practically clashed into each other, neither one of us seeming to have been paying much attention to our surroundings.

When Trevor's grey eyes met my blue ones for the first time in a little over a year, my heart flipped, and not in a good way. The feelings I had for him were long gone, but what made him my ex in the first place still remained, encaging my body in a taunting snare.

We never slept together, thankfully, but even his horrible kissing ability was enough to leave me scarred.

Trevor was the first to break our silence, awkwardly rubbing the back of his head. His brown curls were exactly as I remembered, framing a chubby, white face, and I fought the urge to touch them in order to feel if they were still as silky soft as last time. "Hey, Savannah. Strange seeing you here."

"You knew I'd be here," I clipped, nearly shuddering at how harsh I sounded. This was true though. Those competing *were* public knowledge, after all.

"I know, just..." Trevor fumbled, a sizeable blush coating his cheeks. "It's good to see you. You haven't changed a bit, though your hair...it's so *long*, and—"

"Trevor," I began, though not unkindly. "It's okay. You

don't *have* to ramble."

"Right. Sorry. It's just, it's been so long," Trevor said. "How have you been?"

"It's only been a year, and we live in the same village," I pointed out but then sighed. "Though I've been fine. How about you?"

"Fine." Trevor paused. "I miss you, Sav."

Sav. I nearly recoiled at Trevor's chosen nickname for me, a name that used to elicit a swarm of giddy butterflies in my stomach.

Now, all it did was made me feel nauseous. What sixteen-year-old me even *saw* in him, I'd never understand, especially when we ended things only a few days short of my seventeenth birthday.

Talk about a major buzz kill.

"We weren't good together," I reminded him sternly, which was true. Terrible kissing aside, there had been absolutely no chemistry between us, no sparks flying whenever we were together.

No matter how much we tried to make it work, it seemed we just kept falling flat on our faces.

"I'm not talking about getting back together!" Trevor, to his credit, looked mortified. "You and I deserve so much better, but…I still miss you." He gulped. "As a friend."

A slow pang formed in my gut, one I hadn't noticed before. Because the truth was I missed him as well. I missed the talks we used to have about anything and everything. For a long time, he was the only person who seemed to be able to get through my barriers and take my mind off my seemingly impossible revenge mission. He had been the first person in a long time who truly showed me what it was like to *live*, because he had known loss too.

Trevor once divulged to me how he had a twin, the other half of his soul. But while he had made it out relatively unscathed, his twin was stillborn.

Though he never knew his brother, the loss still affected him to this day, even though his parents continuously told him it wasn't his fault. He was the only one who could possibly understand my guilt, the continuous, nagging thought in my brain scolding me for not doing more to prevent my brother's death.

As if it wasn't his choice to go out.

As if he would've listened to me at all.

I told him to have fun*!*

I shook my head, clearing my mind of the downward spiral it was sure to go down. Today was supposed to be a happy day, my first time taking part in the competition I revered as a child.

I shot Trevor a huge smile, hoping it hid the direction my thoughts were taking. "I miss our friendship too." That, at least, was the truth.

Trevor's face lit up. "Do you want to do something after this?" he asked. "Not a date, but like…as friends?"

I nearly accepted his offer until my mind flashbacked to the boy I had tied up in my attic. Even coming here was a big risk when he could wake up at any moment. "I can't today," I said, and it nearly hurt to watch Trevor's facial expression fall. "But maybe tomorrow?"

Trevor smiled at the ultimatum. "Sure. When and where?"

"Noon at the coffee shop?" I suggested.

"Okay," he said. "See you there."

And that was how the two of us left things as the bell overhead dinged, signaling the competition was about to begin. With hearts full of heartache and the promise of a friendship date on the horizon, the latter of which I would've never seen coming an hour ago.

"Places!" the judge yelled as she scrambled from one area to the next. The judge this year was a short, plump white woman with short hair that was dyed bright pink, wearing a black minidress that hugged her curves in all the right places and a pair of white, too-high stilettos. I nearly gawked in wonder at how she was able to gracefully move around in those heels.

Until the competitors started lining up in a single-file line off to the side, and I had something else to gawk at. Twenty competitors in all, including me, all varying in size and age.

And most of them very intimidating.

I took a quick breath to calm my racing heart before joining them, sliding in between two older men whose faces were set in a grim expression.

Both of them significantly older than me. Suddenly, I felt very small.

"Archer number one, you're up!" the judge, whose name I still didn't know, barked, and just like that, the competition began.

Each of us had been given a number upon registration, and I was number fifteen. At the time, I had been ecstatic to not have been one of the first ones to go, but now, I wished I *had* been, if only so I could get it over with.

Fourteen people ahead of me.

Fourteen performances to make my anxiety grow.

I can do this, I huffed, squaring my shoulders. I trained most of my life to be here, and I deserved this as much as everybody else who was competing.

I *deserved* this.

Just keep hyping yourself up, and everything will be fine.

The first archer to go was a tall woman with medium-brown skin and bleach-blonde locks that fell past her waist. Her lips were pulled straight, eyebrows furrowed in concentration, as she squared her shoulders, narrowing her eyes at the first target.

The buzzer rang, signaling the countdown from five minutes, and she immediately drew her bow, first arrow poised and ready.

There were forty targets in all scattered throughout the square and only five minutes to hit them as accurately as possible. In rapid succession, the woman started firing off arrow after arrow, some piercing the targets dead center while others swung wide of their destination.

I had always been in awe of the archers who could fire

arrows one after the other and most of the time hit their targets. And now, I was finally going to *be* one of them, performing for all to see.

The woman finished with a minute to spare, most targets having arrows protruding out of them. She did a quick bow before returning to her family, paving the way for the next archer to take the stage.

And so, the cycle continued as archer after archer performed to the best of their ability, some only managing around half to three-quarters of the targets before the time ran out. Matilda Brant, who was archer number six, was one of them, only managing a little less than half before she was out of time.

I half-expected Matilda to throw a fit right then and there. After all, it was evident in her face how disappointed she was. Yet instead, she smiled, took a bow, and returned to her beaming parents.

I had no doubt she would let loose later, but for now, she was trying to save face.

Ronna was up next as archer number seven, and to my amazement, she managed to hit all the targets within the timeframe, only a few having struck wide of the center. Her happiness was palpable as her smile reached her eyes, and she curtseyed before leaving the stage.

My heart sank, because there was no way I, logically, could compete with *that* performance, and damn if I let something of Matilda's be better than me.

The next archers' performances were all a blur of

buzzers and firing arrows, faces contorting into one long succession. My head spun with the growing anxiety in my gut, nerves convinced that this was a mistake. That I wasn't good enough to be here.

And then, within the blink of an eye, it was my turn.

And everything suddenly stilled.

I moved forward on stiff legs as if in slow motion as tens of judgmental eyes watched me like a hawk. The square was unbelievably quiet that not even the sound of breathing was heard as I meandered towards the tape, shoulders tense and aching.

I suddenly felt nothing as I reached the starting place. No more heart pounding to the beat of my own anxiety, no butterflies in my gut threatening to drown me, and no palms bursting with sweat.

If I didn't know any better, I would think I was at peace. But I knew better. This was just the calm before the storm.

As soon as my feet met the line of tape, the dam in me broke, and suddenly, I could hear *everything*. The sound of loud cheers coming from my family, the shuffling of feet as people shifted positions, even each individual breath—it all accosted my ears in an endless stream of noise.

But my heart was the worst offender, nearly jumping out of my chest with each beat.

I forced myself to glance up at the faces surrounding me, forcing my body to stay calm and alert. And then, that damn buzzer sounded, and suddenly, my hands weren't my own as they flung for my bow and the first arrow.

I shot arrow after arrow as if something suddenly took a hold of me, wielding my body like a puppet on strings, barely registering if the arrows made their marks. The cheering was now deafening, a constant ringing in my ears that drowned out all other senses.

And when it was finally over—when that buzzer rang out yet again—my eyes focused, and I glanced up over each target.

And to my surprise, I didn't miss a single one, each target having a protruding arrow either on or near the center.

I should've been ecstatic. I should've screamed or cheered or done something aside from just standing there, dumbfounded, as the cheering intensified around me.

I swayed on my feet, light as a feather, as I sauntered off the stage towards my parents. The competition continued on, each contestant after me met with more cheers and praise. Trevor Browning especially, the second to last participant, sauntered to the music of his own screaming mother.

But none of that mattered, not in the slightest. Because finally, I had done what little me had dreamt about for years. I finally became the archer I pictured myself being.

And for a moment, I let myself soak it all in—the sights, the smells, *everything.* For the first time in years, I finally knew what peace felt like.

~*~

I ended up scoring second place with Ronna scoring first, and aside from a trophy, I received a sizable cash prize of one hundred kruts, the official currency of Ebonrowe.

It was more than I ever thought I'd get, so for the moment, I was happy, elated, *excited.* Now, to go home to the elephant in the room, a certain wolf boy who could've been responsible for countless deaths, including my brother's.

I let my parents go ahead and stopped by the butcher to buy a hulking chunk of raw meat with some of my earnings. Then, I returned home, meat carefully wrapped in a plastic bag for the boy who, despite everything, I couldn't let starve. I didn't have it in me to be cruel, even to someone with murderous tendencies.

Even tying him up had been a stretch for me. I never even considered the ramifications of keeping a hostage before. *Was he even a hostage if my reasoning for tying him up was to keep him from harming anybody else?*

Shaking my head, I let loose a laugh. It wasn't like I was planning on torturing him or anything. I just had some questions, and then, I would either let him go or finish the job.

Though considering how fast he healed, it looked more like the latter.

I was expecting a lot of things when I finally returned to the attic. I was expecting him to still be unconscious or perhaps for him to even have gotten *out* of his bindings.

I somewhat expected to be greeted by his wolf form, eyes staring down at me and mouth foaming with saliva.

What I *didn't* expect, however, was to be greeted by wide, fearful eyes and quick, heavy breathing.

A boy who looked scared, not at all like the hulking wolf form I had seen not even twenty-four hours ago.

For a moment, I just stared at him, into his sparkling blue eyes that were a shade lighter than mine. And then, I unwrapped the meat from its packaging and slid it over to him.

"Dinner is served!" I said. And just like that, our interaction descended into further awkwardness.

FOUR

CALLUM

My body felt like it had just been struck by lightning, then run over by a dozen horses when I finally stirred awake, head positioned at an awkward angle that left my neck stiff and tender. Dull, throbbing pain pulsed in my entire body with the occasional sharp jab, and I let out an impromptu groan as I shifted positions on the cold, hard, wooden floor.

My arms were numb, hands tingling with the lack of blood circulation, but when I went to stretch them out, what felt like thick rope bit into the meat of my wrists. I let out a hiss of pain, my body jerking, as I fought to kick out my legs.

Only, they were bound together too, just as tightly, at the ankles. My eyes widened as I stared at the strip of pink flesh that descended lower, hidden by the rope's wiry hairs. And the pants that covered my legs, the bottoms somehow having rolled so they rested a couple inches above my ankles.

Last I remembered, I was in my wolf form, running through the woods with Sammy. And then—

I gasped, sitting bolt upright—or at least, as close to bolt upright as I was going to get in my current position. A white blanket was messily bundled up beside me, and on instinct, I reached for it, only to feel the rope dig into my wrists again.

I wanted to yell. I wanted to scream. But most of all, I wanted to do something that would be seen as unbefitting of a future alpha.

Cry and beg. Because it became more obvious by the minute I had been kidnapped, shot through the shoulder with an arrow before blackness took hold.

Why, I didn't know. There had been the occasional stories of wolves getting kidnapped by rival packs, but we lived far enough away from any that that never really happened.

And they wouldn't use a bow and arrow.

Footsteps sounded below, causing more alarm bells to ring in my mind. I jerked my head—and winced as leather bit into my throat.

A leash. Whoever had kidnapped me wound a leash

around my throat like a damn dog. An impromptu snarl ripped up my throat.

A trap door suddenly slammed open, hands reaching out to grip the floor. I stiffened, thoughts running aimlessly through my head as to who my kidnapper could be, all of the possibilities big, burly men who could pummel me to the ground in an instant.

Instead, what I got was a petite young woman with fair skin and long, blonde hair that fell to her waist. Long, thick bangs swept her forehead, and in her hand was a plastic bag.

Our eyes locked, mine big and fearful, and hers a mixture of shock and confusion. And then, she reached into her plastic bag.

I was prepared for all kinds of torture. Perhaps she had a knife, ready to use it on me for information regarding my pack. Judging by her scent, I could tell right off the bat she was human, and the only thing humans would want would be information.

Especially if she had seen me shift.

All my life, I had been told to be careful. Humans by and large didn't know of our existence, and if we ever accidentally shifted in front of one, we could be picked off and bagged, used for experiments or worse.

I didn't realize there had been a human in the woods last night. If I had known—

The girl took out a wad of paper, carefully unwrapping it before revealing…a chunk of raw meat.

If I wasn't terrified, I would've laughed. Instead of a

knife, she had brought me food. Raw meat, sure, but food nonetheless.

She slid it over to me. "Dinner is served!" she said awkwardly, shifting from one foot to the other as if unsure of what else to do.

Okay, this girl definitely *saw me shift,* I thought. *Otherwise, she wouldn't have brought me raw meat.*

Right?

To her credit, the girl looked like the least threatening person on the planet, but I knew better than most that looks could be deceiving. "Thank you," I rasped, and it was only then when I realized how parched I was. "I know you probably have your reasons for kidnapping me—and believe me, I'm fully prepared to withstand any torture you have in mind—but do you think you could find it in your cold heart to get me some water?"

There. Short, sweet, and to the point.

The girl wrinkled her eyebrows in confusion. "Wait, torture?"

"That's why you kidnapped me, right?" I said evenly. "To torture me for information?"

The girl shook her head, bewildered. "I brought you here because I *thought* you were on death's doorstep!"

I flinched. *She brought me here to try to save me? Then, why was I tied up?* "I don't understand."

"Of course you wouldn't, wolf." The girl sighed. "Whatever. I'll get you some water, and you just...I don't know, wiggle around and eat the nice chunk of meat like a good little doggy."

And then, she spun on her heels—actually *spun*—before exiting the same way she came.

For a moment, I sat there, frozen. If I had any doubts before about the girl knowing what I was, those were long gone as I stared at where she once was. *A good little doggy.* Like I was a pet.

To her credit, though, she didn't seem like she wanted to hurt me. In fact, she seemed just as confused as I was.

So, why was I still tied up?

At that moment, though, it didn't matter. Because as well as thirsty, I was *ravenous*. And somehow, the girl knew that and brought me food when she could've just let me starve.

See how long the wolf shifter could survive when his basic needs were taken away from him.

On instinct, I reached deep inside myself and felt around for my wolf. Usually, he was a calming presence, rubbing up against my insides in silent companionship.

Now, however, he was nowhere in sight, as if he as well was scared, too scared to come out and try to dominate me like he usually did.

Sighing, I shifted my position as best as I could, plopping my face directly on top of the hunk of meat. I took a bite and practically moaned at the flavor that coated my tastebuds. Apparently, all it took was an arrow to the shoulder and an impromptu kidnapping to make raw meat taste like the best thing ever.

I was so engrossed in my meal, I didn't hear the girl's return until she loudly cleared her throat, and I recoiled backwards, slamming my back against the wall.

She gave me a sheepish grin, extending forward a huge dog bowl filled with water. And then, she placed it next to my meal, droplets sloshing up the sides.

I blinked, disbelieving. "I'm not a dog!"

"No, you're just the big, bad wolf who huffed and puffed and blew my whole world down," the girl said bitterly, crossing her arms over her chest.

And that was when I finally sensed it. Anger. The girl was brimming with it, a raging inferno meant to burn me alive.

"What's your name?" the girl suddenly questioned, the drastic change in conversation enough to give me whiplash.

"Excuse me?" I said, dumbfounded.

"Name? What I should call you?" she said. "Somehow, I doubt your parents were stupid enough to name you 'Wolf Boy'."

I nearly snorted. "Thank you for the water."

I thought that would put an end to the conversation, because the last thing I wanted to do was give my kidnapper my name, but it seemed she had other ideas.

"Cool," she said. "Thank me with your name."

I shot her a glare before relenting. After all, one single name wouldn't hurt.

And if I hear her call me Wolf Boy one more time…

"Callum," I said. "Woodsworth. My name is Callum

Woodsworth."

The girl scrunched her face. "That name's not very wolfy."

"Sorry to disappoint."

The girl laughed at that. "Well, Callum Woodsworth, I brought you water, like you asked. Now, you're going to answer some questions."

Here we go, I thought, shaking my head. "You first."

"Excuse me?"

"What's *your* name?" I spat. "Or should I just call you 'The Girl Who Kidnapped Me'?"

"I already told you I didn't kidnap you, at least not intentionally." The girl sighed. "Savannah Collins. There, happy?"

"Immensely."

Savannah shook her head. "You're a real piece of work. You know that, right?"

"And you're the one who shot me with an arrow," I pointed out.

Savannah's face fell at that. "I *thought* I had shot…" Her words faded away. "You know what? Never mind."

But I couldn't let it go, not when she looked like she had kicked a helpless kitten. "Savannah…"

She shot me with a cold glare, her eyes glistening with…*were those tears?* "I thought I had shot a big, hulking wolf, alright?" she snarled, hands tightening into shaking fists. "And instead, I shot a boy! I'm not a killer! I don't kill—" Her voice shook as she blinked back tears. "I'm not a killer."

She was fragile, more fragile than I had originally thought. And yet, I couldn't stop my asshole mouth from saying, "You don't kill people, but wolves are fine, right? Because we're not people?"

"When you *murder* innocent townsfolks—" Savannah began. And then, she stopped, eyes wide, sucking in a gasping breath. As if she didn't *mean* to say that.

A slip of the tongue.

And now, I felt gutted, like *I* had been the one to kick that helpless kitten. "I didn't murder anyone," I said. It was the truth, at least.

But the truth only went so far if she herself didn't even believe me.

"No?" She held up five fingers and started ticking off names. "Mrs. Harlow, Jackson, Edith, Mr. Dunsworth, Mrs. Dunsworth, Mr. Ashcroft, Marilyn, Benny—who was only *five years old*, by the way—"

"Savannah," I said, exasperated, "I have no idea what you're talking about."

"Don't you?" she snapped. "Countless others I didn't even name, *dead*, because you—"

"I don't know what you've heard, but like you, *I don't kill people!*" I yelled, causing her to flinch. Immediately, I softened my voice. "It wasn't me."

None of those names rang a bell to me, but I had no doubt all those deaths truly happened. I knew of Ebonrowe, in the same way everyone in my pack knew of the tiny human village our lands nearly brushed up against. And right now, I was sure that was where I had been taken, forced to face the consequences of crimes I didn't even commit.

"Okay, so let's say it wasn't you," Savannah said carefully. "Who would it have been then? Your friend who got away?"

"What? No!" I shouted, outraged. "Sammy would never—"

"So, the brown wolf has a name too," Savannah mused, "and, I suppose, a human form, just like you?"

"Yes, that kinda comes with the territory of being a wolf *shifter*," I spat, my anger unrecognizable. I didn't even *remember* a time when I was so angry.

Savannah pursed her lips. "How many of you are there?"

"A lot," I said as if the answer was obvious. "More than you can count."

And that didn't even include the shifters of other species. Each animal on the planet had a corresponding shifter form, birthed supposedly from the wombs of different goddesses.

"What about your pack?" Savannah inquired. "Wolves are pack animals, right?"

"I'm not giving you information about my pack!" I snapped, beyond elated. "But I can tell you this. None of us would even *dream* about hurting the humans in your village."

Savannah narrowed her eyes. And then, a sickeningly sweet smile coated her lips. "You'll talk," she ground out. "Eventually, you'll talk."

Then, she turned her back to me, thus leaving me to my pitiful meal, but not before delivering one final blow:

"Tomorrow night is a full moon. I guess we'll know the truth then."

And then, she left, slamming the trap door shut behind her.

Leaving me alone to stew in my thoughts.

FIVE

SAVANNAH

If I had any doubts before of what I had seen in the woods, Callum basically confirmed it. He was some sort of wolf-human hybrid—someone who could take on both forms with nothing more than a mere thought.

Callum claimed he was a wolf shifter, whatever that meant.

Me, I didn't know what I thought. What I *did* know, however, was that Callum irritated me more than anyone else on the planet, with his smooth phrases and smug tone.

He thought I took him with the intention of torturing him. He *literally* thought—

I shook my head, digging my nails into the meat of my palms to keep me grounded. Keep me from going over the edge. *What the hell did I get myself into?*

Scoring second place in the annual archery competition definitely had its perks. For starters, I was no longer a faceless nobody. I was more than the girl who had lost her brother. Even though he had been younger than me, I always lived in the shadow of his death, victim to the occasional pitying glances.

It turned out most people didn't know what to say when faced with grief, so they ignored it like the plague with a few bold enough to approach me and say the wrong thing.

But now, people waved at me, offering me their congratulations and praising my skills as an archer. They were actually complimenting me. *Me*, as if I were some sort of prodigy.

I knew I wasn't, for prodigies didn't get their brothers killed. But it was still nice to bask in the positive attention, a direct contrast to the negativity I was used to.

Plus for once, no one cared where I went. That had been a constant struggle for me for years, people always whispering and gossiping, wondering where the grieving girl was off to this time.

If she was going to visit her brother's grave yet again.

In the early months following my brother's death, I practically lived at his grave's side. But as life continued on, I started going less and less, instead choosing to throw everything I had into archery.

And finally, all my hard work paid off.

Today, I wasn't off to visit my brother's grave or anything like that. Instead, I was heading off to our small library to do some research on my own. If anywhere had information on what Callum was, it was there.

My heart beat frantically in my chest as the library drew closer. I only had a few short hours before it closed for the day, and I was prepared to make every second count.

Starting now.

I jogged the rest of the way to the building's entrance, elated to finally get some answers. But soon, that elation diminished when I saw who was standing outside directly in front of the doors.

Trevor Browning.

I had been so giddy after my performance, I didn't even remember his or how he did. And I was ashamed to admit a part of me felt guilty for that, and that shame hit me at full force as my eyes locked with his.

Locked on his wounded look.

"Hey, Savannah," he greeted as I drew closer, offering me a small smile. A smile that didn't come close to reaching his eyes. "Congratulations."

"Thank you," I said politely, my heart weeping in tune to his sadness. "You were great too."

"Me? Nah." He waved off my compliment. "I didn't even make the top ten."

I shrugged. "You tried your best!" I said. It was the only

thing I could think of to say, but I knew how he felt. If I had scored less than the top ten as well, I would've been sad too.

"So, what're you up to?" Trevor asked, offering another smile for my benefit.

"Oh, you know." I laughed nervously. "Just felt like doing some reading." *Just researching whatever I could find on wolf shifters. No big deal.*

Trevor gave me a once-over, eyes narrowing into slits. "You've never expressed an interest in reading before," he pointed out.

I gulped. This was true, since even before my brother's death, I had always been an outdoorsy person. Sitting in one place for hours on end tended to bore me, so I always found something to do outside. Trevor had always been more of the bookworm.

Which perfectly explained why he was here with a stack of books I for some reason hadn't noticed until now. I, on the other hand, had no excuse, at least not a believable one.

And I couldn't very well tell him the truth. He wouldn't believe me. No one would.

"I thought it was time I picked up a new hobby," I said, matching his smile with one of my own. "Do you have any recommendations?"

"A lot, and I also know if I give them to you, you won't read any of them," Trevor stated matter-of-factly. "I *know* you, Savannah."

Dammit! I cursed, sure my cheeks were blooming every

shade of red imaginable. Even though we had only gone out for a short time, we had been friends long before that. Some may have even argued we had at one point been *best* friends, but those days were long gone.

Something must've shown on my face because Trevor pulled his lips into a frown. "Sav…" he began. "Hey, Sav, what's wrong?"

"What?" I said, for the moment blindsided. "Nothing's wrong!" Aside from the fact I may be harboring a dangerous criminal in my attic, everything was just peachy.

"Your face says otherwise," Trevor stated plainly. "And you're acting weird."

This was bad. Very, very *bad*. For Trevor to immediately see through my act meant I wasn't doing a good enough job of pretending. "I swear, Trevor. Nothing's wrong," I said, hoping he would be a good boy and drop the subject altogether. "We still on for tomorrow?"

Trevor furrowed his brows at the subject change, but he let it slide. "Of course." Then, he lowered his voice to an almost whisper. "You can still talk to me about anything. You know that, right?"

And I *did* know that. He was the only person in the whole world who knew just how much guilt I harbored over my brother's death. Not even my parents knew, for I could never tell them. I was sure they blamed themselves too.

But none of them told him to have fun the night of a full moon. They had all been asleep when he snuck out. I was the one who had caught him red-handed, and I told him to have *fun*.

I was a terrible sister. I should've protected him, but instead, I pushed him to his death. And I would spend the rest of my life trying to make it up to him, even if it meant getting myself killed in the process.

"I know," I said as he skirted by me, his arm brushing against my own. But despite the fact he would understand my own demons better than anyone, I still couldn't bring myself to tell him about Callum. At least not yet.

I watched him move away from me along the cobblestone path that led away from the library. It was only when he finally turned, disappearing from view, that I was finally able to move forward and accomplish what I set out to do.

I had no idea what I would find when I entered the library. But what I didn't expect was something so…quaint. Aside from the librarian, who was currently shelving books off to my right, there was only one other person sitting at one of the tables to my left, bent over a thick book and writing something down on a piece of paper. I didn't remember the person's name, but I'd seen them around town dozens of times.

He looked up at the sound of the entrance bell jingling and gave me a small wave before returning to his book. I returned the gesture and then dashed towards the towering bookshelves, hoping to hide from view. The last thing I needed was someone else distracting me from my mission.

Towards the back, the library had a rather large

collection of nonfiction books, ranging from biographies and autobiographies to basic informative texts concerning different skillsets. I started heading towards where all the animal books were located before changing my mind at the last minute and switching to the fantastical and mythology section.

And it was a good thing I had, because one of the first books I saw was one on mythological beings with a big, gruesome griffin on the cover, its wings snapped out on either side and its beak parted to let out a terrifying screech.

I had never heard the term *wolf shifter* before, and as I looked through the index, it became apparent neither had the author of the book. However, another term stuck out at me, the only one that could even remotely refer to what Callum was.

Werewolf.

But as I flipped to the section, a dark photo of a wolf-like creature standing on two hind legs greeted me. Callum had been on all fours, and though he had been massive, he still resembled a typical wolf, unlike this thing.

I slammed the book shut, sighing in frustration. If Callum was in fact a werewolf, then the author of this book got them all wrong. They *weren't* humanoid-like creatures that stood on two hind legs.

They were true wolves, colossal and magnificent and majestic. They weren't like anything I had ever seen before. And they were also capable of so much death and destruction.

After checking out a few more books and seeing nothing on what Callum was, I gave up and left the library in a daze. The only thing even remotely *close* to what Callum was, was a werewolf, but none of what I read screamed *Callum.*

I was at a loss, fighting the urge to scream at the star-streaked sky. During my time at the library, the sun had completely set, not a streak of warmth remaining.

Leaving me alone to walk home in the cold, brisk air and hope Callum was still where I left him. Good thing my village was normally peaceful and serene.

The moon mocked me the whole way home, just one measly sliver missing from another killing. And that brown wolf was still out there, waiting for the correct time to strike.

At least I had Callum, secured in a way that would hopefully prohibit him from attacking anybody. And what I managed to get out of him led me to believe there were more than two wolf shifters near our village.

Or werewolves, as I was starting to suspect us humans called them.

Hopefully, the fact I had one of their own would deter them from attacking tomorrow. Or perhaps I just doomed Ebonrowe to the worst attack we would ever see.

Or perhaps Callum is telling the truth, and he and his pack truly don't *have anything to do with this.*

I gasped as that thought skirted the back of my mind, the voice sounding like me but at the same time not. Every fiber of my being screamed at me to not trust a word he said, that he *had* to be lying.

But he looked so sincere, his eye contact never wavering. Either he was the best liar on the planet, or he really *was* telling the truth.

I'll know for sure tomorrow night, I told myself, and for a moment, that thought was enough to provide me with comfort, that what I did was justified. The only reason I hadn't outright killed Callum yet was the slim possibility he was innocent, in which case I would have a lot of groveling and apologizing to do.

I hoped he'd understand if it came down to that.

The lights were still on in my house when I finally returned, my father waiting by the door. When he saw me, his face lit up, and he turned his head towards the entrance and screamed, "Donna, she's home! Donna?"

Within a beat, my mother poked her head outside, shooting me an elated smile. "Savannah, honey, where were you?" she inquired before seeming to think better of it. "Never mind. You look like you're freezing! You missed dinner, dear!"

"Were you visiting his grave again?" my father added curiously. "He would've been proud of you, you know. Like your mom and dad are."

I met their smiles with one of my own and said, "Yeah, I told him all about it. About me winning second place." Because letting them believe this white lie was a whole lot better than the truth. They still didn't know what I did each night after they all went to bed.

And whenever I *did* visit Mathias's grave, I talked to him as if he were there with me, so the lie wasn't that far-fetched. Certainly more explainable than me going to the library...

"Trevor came by earlier," my mom said as I was ushered into the house. "He told us to offer you his congratulations, and he left you a little something!"

This surprised me. Trevor must've come here after running into me at the library, knowing I wasn't home yet. And judging by how non-suspicious my parents looked, he for some reason kept my cover.

On the kitchen table was a note and a small, thin book. I crept closer to read the title.

The Chesterfield Curse by Sarah M. Higginbottom. A book of fiction.

"At first, we were confused," my mom said. "After all, you don't read."

"But then, we figured if Trevor gets you to read more, who are we to judge?" my dad added.

But I barely paid any attention to them, instead unfolding the note. And when my eyes landed on his familiar scrawl, I nearly laughed.

Savannah,

You asked me for some recommendations, so I quickly went home and found one for you. This is one of my favorites, and I hope it gives you joy.

-Trevor

P.S. Feel free to keep the book when you're done! I have multiple copies.

~*~

I brought the book to my room, nearly laughing the whole way. After eating my leftover dinner of soup, I stifled a yawn, my body fully prepared to retire for the night.

But my mind wasn't, especially since I still had a date with a so-called wolf shifter in my attic.

After bidding my parents goodnight, I watched them retreated into their shared bedroom on the bottom floor before moving upstairs to my floor. The second floor used to be the floor Mathias and I shared, but ever since his death, it had been mine and mine alone. My parents even rarely went up there anymore, unable to be in such close proximity to what used to be my brother's room.

Which made the attic the perfect place to house Callum. There was no way my parents would suspect a thing.

I used to go into Mathias's room frequently, as if his ghost still lingered within its walls. But that had stopped quite some time ago, when anger and revenge replaced the sadness I was desperately clinging to.

I stared at the stairs that led to the trap door for a

moment, silence surrounding me as I strained to hear a single sound. But there was nothing.

Taking a deep breath, I steeled my resolve and slowly approached the stairs. Callum was still there. He *had* to be, because the alternative was too much to think about.

I climbed the stairs slowly, finally reaching the top and unlocking the hatch. Then, I pushed the door open slowly and peeked my head through, pulling the chain above my head so light flooded the attic.

And there was Callum, just where I left him, still bound, much to my relief.

Staring at the wooden floor, evidently refusing to meet my gaze. But it wasn't fear this time that ailed him, which seemed to shock me more than I'd like to admit.

It was anger. Pure, unadulterated anger.

And it was directed at me.

SIX

CALLUM

The first time I heard about Ebonrowe, I had been ten years old. My mom and dad sat me down and told me about the humans who lived in a small, rural village that bordered pack lands. They told us that a long time ago, Alonsia bestowed upon her children a purpose. We were to protect humans at all cost, for they had at once been believed to be the catalysts for a better world. But those days ended when the humans ultimately betrayed us, killing and enslaving our people until we were nothing but vessels for their growing evil. With the help of the other goddesses, Alonsia freed us and sent all shifter species on a path of separation and solitude.

For centuries, that was how we lived, having separate but peaceful lives from the humans who would wish us harm at a moment's notice. And as punishment, Alonsia and the other goddesses erased human memory of all supernatural species. It was said we had to be extremely careful after that, never allowing a human to see that we were anything but lest history repeated itself.

And due to my foolish actions, it did, landing me at the feet of a girl who was accusing me of murder. A girl who was so convinced *I* was the monster, she had no idea what her own race was capable of.

I didn't know what felt worse, the fact she wouldn't even hear me out or the fact she apparently brought me here to save me, only to tie me up and leave me to rot in the end. Even now, an itch clawed its way through my skin, begging to be scratched.

I needed to shift. But my wolf was still nowhere to be found.

"Okay, buddy," I said under my breath. "I need you to listen to me for once. Come out so we can finally be done with this whole charade."

I rarely spoke to my wolf, and when I did, it was usually in an effort to coax him out and get him to listen for once in our shared life. But something was different this time. Usually, my wolf ignored me out of defiance, but this time, it was something else.

At first, I thought it was fear, but that didn't seem right, considering I wasn't even that fearful anymore. If

Savannah had wanted to hurt me, she would've done so by now.

Instead, she accused me of murder and said some bullshit about the full moon, as if that would solve anything.

Shifter species were at their strongest during the full moon, yes. But we didn't *need* it to shift, and to think I would go out and murder—

A light soon flickered on, and Savannah's damn blonde head popped up from the trap door. Gripping the sides of the entrance, she pulled herself up easily, closing the door behind her.

And then, she went and plopped herself down in front of me, crossing her legs and gazing at me with a curious expression.

For a moment, none of us spoke. Then…

"What are you doing here?" I spat coldly, refusing to meet her eyes. "Come to gawk at the supposed murderer some more?"

"No," Savannah clipped. Short and sweet and to the point.

And also damn confusing and irritating.

"Change your mind about torturing me?" I shot her a mischievous smile, which she didn't return.

Savannah sighed. "I admit, you're not at all what I was expecting."

"And what exactly *were* you expecting?" I quipped.

Savannah cocked her head to the side. "I'm surprised you haven't tried to shift and escape yet."

"Is that really what you want to see? A big, hulking wolf in your attic?"

"No!" Savannah shook her head. "But I still expected more of an effort from someone who murdered—"

"That hasn't been proven."

"Oh, no?" Savannah chuckled. "Every night, I go out searching, waiting for the beast to finally reveal itself to me so I can finally put it down. And then, one night, I find you, and you just expect me to believe that was all mere coincidence?"

"I'm just saying you shouldn't tamper with things you barely understand," I growled. And that was when I finally felt it, a slight stirring in my gut.

My wolf had finally awoken, and he was still currently rattling around in his skeletal cage.

But now, I was tamping *him* down, refusing to give Savannah the satisfaction of a full shift. I didn't know why, but suddenly, proving my innocence to this girl made it to the top of my priorities list.

"Again, why are you here?" I repeated, exasperated. "Did you come just to mock me?"

Savannah sighed. "I thought you could use some company."

This shocked me, for it meant not even Savannah was convinced of the lies she had been spouting. Either that, or she had a death wish, because no sane person would choose to voluntarily spend time with a supposed killer.

Especially one who could break out of these bindings

with ease, if only I would just shift.

No! I scolded myself, because if I did so and ended up accidentally hurting her, I would be no better than what she had accused me of doing.

Pain, trauma, and sadness were packed together, trapped in Savannah's tiny form. Something drastic must've happened to her to make her this cold and distant.

It wasn't my place to pry, wasn't my place to help her through this pain. But that didn't mean I couldn't enjoy her company, even if her plans to trap me here had been misguided.

"I went to the library this evening," Savannah said suddenly. "I found nothing on you."

I fought the urge to shake my head. "As you wouldn't."

"And why is that?"

"Humans don't exactly know about us," I said. "We tend to keep our distance."

"Except when you're murdering us, you mean."

I gave an exasperated sigh. "Savannah—"

"Callum," she said mockingly.

If my hands had been free, I was sure my face would've been between them right now. And then, I said something I probably shouldn't have. "If you truly believed the words you were spouting, you would've ended me already."

The air suddenly shifted, tension seeping through every pore of Savannah's being. It was evident I hit the nail on the bullet, but it seemed she didn't want me to know that.

If I had been scared of her before, the look she shot me

would've had me absolutely terrified. As it was, her eyes practically burned as they raked over my form.

And then, she did something I didn't expect. She sighed, dropping her head so it rested in her hands. "I don't want it to be true," she confessed, her voice muffled. "But the evidence suggests—"

"What evidence?" I interrupted, daring to scoot as close to her as my bindings would allow. "All you've told me so far are suspicions!"

"Suspicions founded in fact!" Savannah snapped, tearing her head away from her hands so fast I nearly jumped. "These murders are animal caused! I've *seen* the bodies!"

Her voice broke on the last word, her body trembling with grief. This girl had been through more than most people her age, and not for the first time, my heart broke for her. But even though it did, nothing excused her actions.

"Savannah," I said, quieter this time. This was the second time I had seen my kidnapper in such a vulnerable state, and I didn't know what to make of it.

But then, she did something completely unexpected. She flung her arms around me as if we were friends and not two strangers who had just met under weird circumstances, burying her tear-soaked face in the crook of my neck as she sobbed quietly.

And I, not knowing what else to do, let her be, leaning forward so she could wrap even more of herself around me. For a moment, it seemed she forgot that she was supposed to hate me, instead finding comfort in the only other person in the room.

Just as suddenly as she embraced me, she flung herself back as if my touch scorched her, her eyes wild with embarrassment. "You don't understand," she hissed, unable to hide the tremble in her voice as she blotted her puffy eyes with the back of her sleeve. "If not you, I'd go back to square one again, and I can't! I just can't!"

"Savannah," I repeated, trying to get through to her one more time. Trying to reach her more rational side.

And then, a brief flash of something appeared in her eyes, something that looked a lot like...*grief.*

Suddenly, everything began to make sense. All the pieces finally fell into place. Suddenly, I had an explanation for why this girl was so frantic.

This animal, whatever it was, took someone important from her. It would explain why she was so desperate to find it and put it into the ground. It would also explain why she had been in the woods last night and almost killed me with one of her arrows.

But I was not the animal she was looking for, nor was it anyone else in my pack.

"Savannah, I know you're grieving for a loss you still haven't fully accepted," I began, talking to her like one would do a small, wounded animal. "But—"

Savannah's expression hardened in an instant. "You know *nothing* of what you're talking about!" she spat.

"I know you're hurting—and believe me when I say

what you're feeling is completely justified—but I'm not what—"

"Don't you *dare* finish that sentence," Savannah snarled. "You. Know. *Nothing.*"

"I know you're having doubts," I said, "and you're not ready for the possibility of being wrong."

That seemed to be the last straw for her, for in an instant, Savannah shoved herself off the floor, her eyes staring daggers at me as she towered over me. "You know, I *thought* I was doing a good thing keeping you company, but it seems I was wrong." And then, she turned on her heels and proceeded to leave me alone once again.

But for once, I couldn't just let her leave, not after she had shown me her vulnerable side twice now. "Savannah!" I called out, watching as she stiffened when I said her name.

She didn't turn around, but she *had* paused, which was good enough for me. It meant she was listening.

"Let me help you," I said, surprised to find I was actually earnest in my offer. Despite what she had done, there was a justifiable reason behind it, and if the roles had been reversed, I was sure I would've done the same. "I know these woods like the back of my hand. Let me help you find some closure."

Savannah balled her hands into trembling fists. "Your innocence hasn't been proven yet, wolf," she snarled, bending over to open the trap door. "I don't need or want your help."

And then, she turned off the light and leapt through the

opening, banging the door shut behind her. Leaving me alone in utter darkness.

SEVEN

SAVANNAH

I didn't sleep well that night, my dreams plagued with nightmares of my brother as the beast sunk its hefty jaws into him again and again while I helplessly watched from the sidelines. And when I woke up, it was to the sound of screaming, body drenched in sweat.

Last night was the first night in a long time I didn't go hunting, the first night I slept through, stuck in my perpetual nightmare. I had nearly forgotten the feeling of the sun on my face as it streamed its light through my window or the warmth my covers provided as I hugged them to my chin.

But I hadn't forgotten last night, my arms around

Callum in a moment of weakness as I sobbed into his shoulder. For some reason, he was able to see right through me, piecing together my motivation like it was a mere puzzle. And not only that, but he had offered me *help*. My brother's supposed killer, offering me help.

And now, I was at a standstill between believing his words and believing my gut, and my gut was losing. Whenever I visited him, my guard fractured just a little more, which was very dangerous if he truly *was* the killer.

I was the one who had tied him up, and he offered me comfort in return. *Perhaps I* was *the monster in this relationship...*

The morning passed by rather slowly. By the time I had made my way downstairs, my parents had already left for work. After scouring the fridge for some leftover meat, I briefly visited Callum to give him his breakfast. He was still asleep, curled onto his side, his soft snores infiltrating the quiet space.

For a few seconds, I watched him sleep, my resolve shattering just a little bit more. He didn't look any bit the monster I spent most of my life picturing my brother's killer as being. Instead, he looked like any other human, and if I hadn't seen what I did in the woods, I probably would've mistaken him as one.

I left before more of my resolve broke, reminding myself that until tonight, I wouldn't know for sure. Tonight was the next full moon, and it was guaranteed someone was going to die unless I managed to put a stop to it.

And if I was wrong…

Stop thinking that way! I scolded myself, making my way back to the kitchen to find myself something to eat. I couldn't afford to be wrong, because if I was, more people would die.

And I'd have one very pissed off wolf shifter to contend with.

At noon, I made my way to the coffee shop, where Trevor and I promised to meet each other. The air was freezing as we headed closer to winter, causing me to pull my coat tighter around my small frame.

Trevor was already there when I finally arrived, casually sipping a coffee at a small table by one of the windows, a half-eaten cheese pastry pushed to the left. He looked up as I entered, smiling and waving when he saw me. I gave him a smile and a wave in return before making my way to the counter.

I ended up ordering a white chocolate latte with a cinnamon donut, and after five minutes, I went to join him with my purchases in hand.

"What'd you get?' I greeted as I sat down, motioning towards his coffee with my shoulder.

"Caramel macchiato," Trevor said. "You?"

"White chocolate latte." I took a bite of donut, savoring the way the cinnamon dusted my tongue in sweet goodness.

Trevor barked out a laugh. "Some things never change, do they, Savannah?"

"Why try new things if there's a chance you're not

going to like it?" I quipped, raising my cup and taking a huge sip. The drink warmed me up instantly, spreading throughout my body with pleasure. I sighed, content, before going for another sip.

This had always been my go-to drink whenever Trevor and I came here in the old days. Whereas Trevor always varied his drinks, I kept to the same thing, not bothering to try something I may not like as much.

"Spoken like true stubbornness," Trevor said lightheartedly before leaning forward. "Did you get my present?"

"The book? Yeah, I did. Though I admit I'm kinda surprised," I admitted.

Trevor shrugged. "I figured there was a slim chance you were serious, so I went for it." He took a sip of his drink. "Just promise me you'll read it. I expect a full report when you're done."

"Noted!" I laughed before taking another bite of donut.

With every second that passed, I felt my tension easing as the scene became more familiar around me. When Trevor and I started dating, we stopped hanging out as mere friends and did more of what we deemed were couple-y things. But sitting here, just talking as old friends, was nice in a way I couldn't describe. I missed Trevor as a friend, and though I would never get back together with him, I couldn't see myself completely cutting him off from my life.

He had been the only one who treated me as an actual person, someone separate from my dead brother's shadow.

And I regretted ever letting him go.

"Sav?" Trevor gazed into my eyes curiously, as if he had just said something and expected a response back.

I shook my head. "I'm sorry, what?"

"I asked if you remembered the last time we came here."

"Oh. Of course," I said. It had been just before we became a couple, one of our last hangouts as friends. "You dared me to try the cinnamon spice cappuccino, which was *awful*, by the way!" That day, I had learned I did *not* mix well with spicy things. It was so bad, I nearly spat the entire thing out on Trevor.

Trevor laughed. "It was worth it to see your face!"

I shook my head, unable to hide the smile that blossomed on my lips. "Whoever thought it was a good idea to mix cinnamon and spice in the same drink should be tried for blasphemy!"

"Somehow, I don't think that's what 'blasphemy' entails."

"Of course it does!" I argued. "That drink was purely blasphemous!"

Trevor gave one more hearty laugh before the smile disappeared from his face. "Savannah…"

I didn't realize I had stopped smiling until nervous butterflies started appearing in my stomach. And suddenly, our moment of lightheartedness abruptly ended.

"Savannah, I…I'm sorry," Trevor said, nervously chewing on his bottom lip. "I should never have let you go."

"Trevor, we were *terrible* together," I reminded him,

because it was the truth. As friends, we were great, but as lovers, less so.

"That's not what I meant!" Trevor argued, but this time, I could see the lie clearly in his eyes. He missed me, though not in a best friend sort-of way. He had lied to me to get me here with the hope of winning me back. And my heart was having none of it.

You already belong to someone else, it whispered in my gut, but that couldn't be right either. There was no one else in my life right now except—

"Callum!" I suddenly blurted without thinking, my eyes going wide as my heart beat in tune to his name. Suddenly, flashes of my arms going around him, his body holding me up as I cried into his shoulder, accosted me, drowning me in an endless current of feelings I couldn't possess. *No!* I screamed at my traitorous heart. After all, he was the enemy, and we had only *just* met.

A flash of hurt and confusion appeared in Trevor's eyes. "Who the hell is Callum?" he demanded.

Suddenly, I felt like I had been backed into a corner, about to drown in a sea of white blonde hair and piercing blue eyes. "No one!" I screamed, a lot louder than I meant to. "He's no one!"

"He doesn't *sound* like—"

"I have to go," I said suddenly. "Thank you for meeting with me!" Then, I ran out of there with my half-eaten donut and half-drunk coffee so fast, I didn't give Trevor the chance to protest.

He and I were permanently over. That was the only thing I was sure about. Now, what to do with Callum, on the other hand…

"Fuck!" I screamed, throwing open the door to my house. This was bad. Very, very bad. Worse than running into Trevor at the library.

Callum was the *enemy*! I hoped if I said it enough times, my heart would listen, but even I was having a hard time denying *something* was there when he held me.

His skin was so gentle and soft, propping me up like I would crumble at any moment. And I wanted nothing more than to be back at his side, where I felt safe and cared for.

Where I felt like nothing could hurt me for the first time in my life.

Without giving my actions a second thought, I finished off my donut and coffee before throwing the wrapper and cup in the trash. Then, I marched upstairs, my heart leading the way, before my brain finally caught up to me and stopped me.

I was at war with my body, and I had no idea why.

"Fuckity fuck!" I gave one final scream to whoever would listen before marching up the rest of the stairs and staring at the entrance to the attic.

Callum had to be awake by now. Would he let me hold him like last time? Or would he push me away after I had pushed *him* away?

Only one way to find out…

Squaring my shoulders, I marched to the trap door and

yanked it open, eliciting a loud bang when the door made contact with the wooden floor. I winced at the sound, but only for a short while, before pulling myself up into the attic.

Where a wide-eyed Callum stared at me, watching as I pulled myself up like a feral demon out of hell. And perhaps to him, I still *was* that demon, since I had been the one to tie him up.

Speaking of being tied up...

His arms were still behind his back, muscles straining against the shirt I lent him. I itched to run my fingers over those muscles, feeling as they flexed beneath my touch.

I wanted more than his body propping me up. I wanted him to actually hold me and whisper promises that everything would be okay and that we would find my brother's killer together.

The only thing stopping me was there was still the possibility of him *being* the killer, and if I untied any part of him now, there was a chance he would not hesitate to kill me. *Especially* when the full moon finally came.

I marched over to him with purpose, watching as he recoiled as I went near him. If I wasn't currently so fucked in the head, I would've laughed at his reaction.

"Finally change your mind about torturing me?" Callum questioned only semi-jokingly. There was true fear in his eyes this time, more than there had ever been before.

"If I said yes, would you stop whining?" I huffed, spearing him with a cold and dark look that made him squirm even more. "I'm just here to observe you, see if there are any changes as the full moon draws closer."

"Nothing's going to happen!" Callum protested. "I already told you—"

"Forgive me if I say what comes out of your mouth right now doesn't mean shit when my village is dealing with an epidemic older than time itself!" I snapped, digging my nails into the meat of my palm. Unbeknownst to him, my anger this time wasn't directed at him at all but was instead a direct product of the war raging on inside my body.

I wanted his comfort, but at the same time, I craved justice. And the only way I would get it was if he and everyone else in his pack met an untimely demise. *How fucked is that?*

"My offer still stands," Callum said boldly. "I can see your turmoil clear as day, and I want to help you!"

"Why?" I snapped. "After what I've done?"

"I know you're upset, but this isn't the answer," Callum tried again. "Let me go, and I promise—"

Before I knew what I was doing, my heart won, and I collapsed against him, burying my face into his chest. He smelled nice, like a combination of musk and cedarwood, further allowing my heart to build up a case against my brain.

"I don't know what's happening to me," I whispered softly in between sobs. "It's like I can't stop thinking about you, and what happened last night—"

"Savannah," Callum said softly, my name sounding like

smooth butter coming from his lips. And then, his shoulders sagged as he leaned forward, resting his chin on the crook of my neck.

His version of holding me as I sobbed, since his wrists were still bound.

I didn't know why he allowed himself to comfort me when I had been so mean to him. Any other person would've said something mean right back, but not Callum. Instead, he let me use him as my beacon, the only thing holding me together.

I should've hated him for what he was and what he could've done. But surprisingly enough, I didn't. Perhaps he was as much a victim in all of this as I was.

"Your hair smells like apples," Callum whispered against my neck, sending shivers down my spine. He let out a bitter laugh. "How come I haven't noticed that before?"

"Because I'm your captor meant to torture you for information," I joked through wracking sobs. "Is that a bad thing?"

"No. I like apples. It reminds me of home."

I suddenly pulled back and met Callum's gaze. "What's home like?"

"It's beautiful. Positively breathtaking," he said just inches from my lips. "We built our homes from the nature that surrounds us, allowing us to become one with the earth. Perhaps someday, you could visit. That is, if you promise not to kill any of us."

Hearing Callum say that reminded me of just how close

we were, how much heat our bodies were producing. Against my own body's wishes, I scooted back, horrified at what I had just done. Once again, I had taken comfort in a suspected murderer.

I truly am *fucked!*

"Savannah?" Callum questioned, confusion marring his brow.

But I barely heard him as my heart and brain battled it out once again. "I've gotta go," I suddenly said, making a dash towards the attic entrance. "I'll be back tonight."

And then, before I could catch wind of Callum's protests, I practically threw myself into the opening and slammed the trap door shut with a loud clang.

EIGHT

CALLUM

I had never been one to believe in fated mates, but in that moment, I was sure that was what I was experiencing with Savannah. Which was impossible. Because she was human, and I was a wolf shifter. But nonetheless, it burned when she abruptly tore herself away from me as if actively fighting against herself.

Because she couldn't be mated to a killer, right?

I wanted to laugh. I wanted to scream. But mostly, I wanted to cry, because only the universe would be so cruel as to set me up with someone who could barely stand me. Someone who wasn't even a wolf shifter, at that.

I liked to think Alonsia wouldn't be this cruel, that there was a method to her madness. Perhaps this was her way of saying I *wouldn't* die tonight and the girl would finally come to her senses and spare me. And then, I'd help her get the closure she deserved.

In the beginning, fated mates, or *soul* mates, were what Alonsia and the other shifter goddesses did to test our compatibility with other shifters. Those who were deemed fated mates mated for life, and it was said everyone had one in this world. Normally, they were usually reserved for shifters of the same species, but occasionally, they would occur between two different shifter species.

I had never heard of a case, however, where a shifter was fated to a human. I was sure that could've happened at one point, perhaps when humans still knew of our existence before they turned on us, but never now. The risk would've been too great.

And now, as if by a cruel twist of fate, I was fated to my kidnapper, to the girl who threatened me because she thought I was responsible for murdering her people.

I pictured Alonsia laughing at me from her perch high in the clouds, laughing at the child she just screwed over. Perhaps this was punishment for being a weak heir, unable to control my wolf.

But then, I thought of how she felt against me, how for a moment, it was like everything was right in the world.

The urge to scream clogged my throat, and before I could stop myself, a loud yell clawed its way out of my mouth and rattled the walls. And it felt *good* to let all my frustrations go in that one feral sound, surrounding the otherwise quiet space with noise.

I screamed until my throat hurt in protest, until the sun finally set, bathing the attic in darkness. I screamed until I couldn't scream anymore, when the swift slamming of an attic door abruptly cut off any future sound, and a very pissed-off Savannah infiltrated the small space.

"Could you be any louder?" she whined, dragging with her what looked like a sleeping bag, a pillow, a small, lit lantern, a medium-sized kitchen knife, and her signature bow and arrows. "You're lucky my parents aren't home yet!"

"Wait—parents?" I inquired, watching with wide eyes as she made a makeshift camp in the center of the room. "And what's with the weapons?"

"You didn't think I lived in this big, old house by myself, did you?" Savannah spread out the sleeping bag before plopping herself on it, crossing her legs underneath her tiny frame. She blatantly ignored my second question, which did nothing to lessen my uneasiness.

"And the weapons?" I prompted again with a single eyebrow raised.

"Tonight is a full moon," Savannah deadpanned, patting the handle of the knife beside her. "I need to be prepared in case you go all psycho wolf on me."

And just like that, we were back to our usual banter. I didn't know how I felt about that. "And the other stuff?"

She moved the lantern over to her right and stretched her legs. The soft glow from the lantern gave the attic an almost homey feel to it, causing shadows to flicker on the walls in tune to its dance.

"I thought we could have a sleepover." Savannah grinned mischievously. "Stay up really, really late. Tell each other some ghost stories. Maybe even have a pillow fight…" Her eyes trailed down to where my arms disappeared behind my back. "Well, maybe not a pillow fight *per se*, unless you're keen on using your mouth."

I scowled. "No, thank you."

"Boo, you're no fun!" Savannah collapsed onto her sleeping bag, kicking her legs high into the air. "And here I was, thinking the point of hostages was to entertain me."

"Sorry to disappoint," I grumbled, "but if you need entertainment, I could sing for you." Very, very badly, but I could sing nonetheless.

Savannah scrunched up her face. "No, thank you."

"That's what I thought."

An awkward beat of silence stretched between us, the only sounds our steady breathing and my thumping heart. Moonlight started streaming through the window, blanketing the room in a dim, ethereal glow.

Savannah's long hair fanned out from her head, surrounding her in a blonde halo. I yearned to reach out and run my fingers through it to find out whether it was as soft as it looked. My muscles ached, watching the rise and fall of her chest.

The tough persona the girl exhibited was all an act, hiding a person whose grief and sorrow defined them. Now that I had gotten to know her a little, it was clear as day, the walls she built around herself slowly chipping away to let pieces of who she was shine through.

"A long time ago, in this very same village, a house resided deep into the woods," I began, smiling as Savannah turned her head, meeting my gaze with a curious one of her own. "No one went near it, for those who did were never heard from again."

"What are you doing?" Savannah questioned, furrowing her brows.

"Telling a ghost story," I said nonchalantly. "Like you told me to."

"I didn't *tell* you to do anything!"

Shaking my head, I tsked. "Do you want me to tell the story or not?"

"Fine. Whatever," Savannah casually waved her hands about. "But if this story has a lame ending, I reserve the right to smack you."

"How is that any different than normal?" I teased, and she shot me a glare. "Okay, okay. So, this house, people disappeared when they went near it, yadda, yadda, yadda. Then one day, a brave, young boy—"

"Yawn," Savannah said. "Why does it have to be a boy?"

"Fine. A brave, young *girl*—"

"Still *yaaaaaaaaawn*." Savannah rolled onto her side, shooting me a cheeky grin. "Why does it have to be a person at all?"

I barked out a laugh. "Excuse me?"

Savannah curled into a ball, still staring at me with those beady, innocent eyes. "Here, let me try." She paused. "A house resided deep in the woods no one went near for fear of disappearing, blah, blah, blah. Then one day, a handsome, courageous dragon—"

I nearly choked, my eyes growing as big as saucers. "A *dragon*? Like, the giant flying lizards who shoot fire out of their mouths? *That* kind of dragon?" I shook my head. "What business does a creature like that have being in a ghost story?"

"Dragons are haunted by ghosts too!" Savannah protested, only somewhat serious. "Besides, who's telling the story here?"

"It was supposed to be me!"

"Well, your story was boring, so I figured I'd spice it up a bit." Savannah grinned like she was the most innocent girl on the planet.

I may have only known her for about two days, but this girl was anything *but* innocent. There was a side to her I guessed not a lot of people saw, the side that could completely let go and just live.

"Now, where was I?" She rolled off her sleeping bag, staring up at me with the biggest doe eyes on the planet. "Ah, yes. This dragon was the most handsome and the most courageous throughout the entire village. And so, he was commissioned to investigate the house, but when he got there, do you know what he found?"

I leaned forward. "No, nor do I particularly *want* to know."

"Nothing," Savannah deadpanned, blinking up at me with those big eyes of hers. "Absolutely nothing."

"Then, what was the point of—"

"And then, boom! Ghosts started coming out of nowhere, aiming for the dragon's eyes!" Savannah yelled, clapping her hands for extra emphasis. "And the big, burly, courageous dragon took one look at them and was like, 'Nope, I'm out!' So, he dashed to the entrance, but the ghosts were quicker than him. They surrounded him and started to force-feed him asparagus!"

I raised an eyebrow. "Asparagus? Really?"

"I'm not done yet!" Savannah snapped. "So then, the dragon actually turns *into* an asparagus! And the ghosts start munching on him! And that poor, poor dragon was never seen or heard from again. The end!"

I groaned. "How was that any better than my story?"

"Because yours would've been predictable," Savannah said as if the answer was the most obvious in the world. "Mine wasn't."

"Yours was stupid."

"I prefer the term magnificent. A true masterpiece!" She chuckled and then pulled her lips into a frown. "The full moon should be well in the sky by now."

I chuckled along with her. "And?"

"You're not turning."

"First of all, the term is *shifting*," I corrected her. "Second of all, I told you I had nothing to do with—"

"The night is still young," Savannah said, her eyes narrowing into slits. "There's still time."

I scoffed. "And I suppose you're going to stay up all night to try to catch me in the act?"

Savannah scooted closer to me, her head practically in my lap. "That's right!" she gloated, beaming. "Pretty soon, you'll crack. They always do."

"Sorry to disappoint you, but you'll find nothing."

"That's what you *want* me to think." Savannah winked and then brought her hands to her mouth to stifle a yawn. "In any case, I'll be waiting with open arms to say, 'I knew it!'"

I shook my head, exasperated. "Go to sleep, Savannah. You're tired."

"So you can slit my throat in the middle of the night? No thanks." Savannah paused. "No, I think I'm going to stay right here and watch you like a hawk."

"Watch like a hawk all you want." I shifted my position so I was lying on my side, the most comfortable I could be with these bindings. "I'm going to sleep."

I closed my eyes, hearing Savannah shuffle around a bit, possibly to get into a more comfortable position. And then, I fell asleep.

NINE

SAVANNAH

Light was streaming through the attic windows, yanking me out of whatever dreamscape I had found myself in. The soft chirping of birds infiltrated my eardrums as I opened one eye and then the other.

Only to be met with a wall of well-defined chest. *Shit!*

As quickly as I could, I scrambled back as far as I was able to, scrunching up the sleeping bag I had brought for myself but then never used. A sleeping bag I never even *intended* to use, because I had anticipated watching Callum all night.

Instead, *he* had been my sleeping bag, his body cradling my own in a bed of warmth only *he* could produce. And that was when it finally hit me.

I fell asleep next to Callum Woodsworth. I practically *slept* on a hulking wolf shifter who could've eaten me sometime during the night, and I wouldn't have known!

I slept next to my brother's murderer, my traitorous mind reminded me. *I betrayed Mathias!*

But looking at Callum now, with the sunlight illuminating his pale features, he didn't *look* dangerous. And if he had gone on a murderous rampage last night, then…why was I still alive?

Because he was telling the truth, you fool!

Fuck!

I shook my head, disheveled, blonde hair falling in my face, as I watched the wolf shifter slumber. There was no way he was innocent. He *couldn't* have been innocent.

The only possible explanation I thought was perhaps there were no murders last night. Perhaps in his twisted scheme to deceive me, he purposely didn't shift and kill anyone last night.

I went downstairs before Callum had a chance to wake up, even more confused than ever. After all, what motivation could he possibly have to deceive me? But then, as I was grabbing a couple hard-boiled eggs out of the fridge for myself, that blaring alarm sounded, and that was when I knew I was wrong.

My insides immediately filled with dread.

I was wrong!

Without wasting a beat, I devoured the eggs and laced up my boots by the backdoor. And then, I pushed my way outside and started running towards the town square, the place people gathered when they were about to mourn a loss.

I ran as fast as my legs could handle, needing to see for myself who was killed. Needing to see for myself that I was wrong about Callum.

Because he hadn't shifted once during the night. If he had, I would've been dead too.

I barely felt the biting cold of the air as I ran, barely felt the strain in my lungs with each short breath I took. I barely felt much of anything, my mind focused on one thing and one thing only.

This can't be happening!

I was the Huntress. I was supposed to prevent this from happening, and I failed. Another death was added to Ebonrowe's tally because I was wrong.

I'm so goddamn stupid!

The familiar sight of gathered people in the town square sent a wave of déjà-vu crashing through me. For a moment, I was breathless as I slowed my pace to a trot, searching the faces to see who was accounted for. I immediately saw Mom and Dad, who were huddled next to each other. Mom was struggling to hold back tears while Dad held her in silent comfort. I wasn't proud of it, but relief surged through me that they weren't the next victims.

Then, I saw Trevor, standing off to the right with his family. His face was set in a grim expression, eyes red and puffy from the tears he failed to hold back.

I even saw Ronna and Briana, who were frozen stiff, eyes wide open and mouths forming a capital O, as if they were in shock. I crept closer, and the crowd instantly parted to let me through.

I immediately knew why everyone was in shock. In the center of the square were five bodies, all with fresh, gaping wounds that still leaked blood. But that wasn't what sent my heart racing, my lungs screaming for air and panic beginning to take hold.

It was the third body, the one Ronna and Briana were staring at.

The body of Matilda Brant.

~*~

I was sure of a lot of things. I was sure of archery, of the way the bow naturally fit in my grasp. I was sure of my parents' love for me, and even that of Trevor. And I was sure of my absolute hatred for Matilda Brant and her followers. And usually, I was sure of myself, of my gut instincts, which had never steered me wrong before.

But now, none of those things mattered. Because I had never felt so unsure of myself in my life.

Doubt was a fickle thing, slowly creeping in and poisoning the mind with negativity. And I was starting to doubt it all—my abilities as an archer, my gut, and even if I was *deserving* of love. It all swirled around in my brain in an endless hurricane of torment that left me gasping for just the slightest bit of relief.

Unfortunately for me, however, relief never came as I crashed to the ground, my head spinning as Matilda's face leered at me over and over again.

Taunting me.

Bile rose in my throat. Matilda Brant was now dead, having been slain by our village's curse. And now, her face haunted me, shouting every single profanity at me she could. It didn't matter that she was a bully. All that mattered was that she was gone, and I failed to prevent her death.

A cool washcloth was placed on my head, eliciting a groan from my throat. My entire body ached, sharp jabs of pain spearing my torso like the sharp end of a knife. The panic was gone, replaced by a sense of tiredness, a desire to sleep for an eternity.

My head was cradled in the soft fabric of a pillow, piles of sheets cocooning my body on the softest bed I had ever felt. A groan escaped my lips as pain mixed with pleasure, and I closed my eyes tight against the fluorescent lights of the room I was in.

I didn't remember all the details of how I got to that room. In my panic-induced state, all I remembered were blurred faces as they peered down at me, cold fingers probing at my skin as they assessed me. And then, I remembered being carried, my vision fading in and out as Matilda leered at me from the beyond, whispering threats that I would be next. That I would join my brother soon in death.

But I wasn't dead. That much, I knew. The pounding in my ears could only be the sound that signaled I was very much alive. And in that moment, I wished I wasn't. I wished I hadn't survived when so many others had their lives cut short.

Especially since I was a failure. I had let them all down.

I heard the sound of people talking, but I couldn't make anything out. Blurred figures moved in and out of my vision, coming and going as they pleased. My bed dipped as a significant weight plopped down on it, hair that wasn't my own tickling my face as whoever it was peered at me.

"Savannah?" God, even the sound of my *name* was muffled, a soft whimper escaping my throat at the frustration. The pounding of my head threatened to pull me under once again, but I held on, refusing to go back to the dark space that was my mind.

"Savannah!" the voice repeated, more alarmed. "Savannah, can you hear me?"

"Mmmmhmmmm," I hummed as I attempted to nod. However, my neck didn't respond, my limbs like dead weights, holding me down like restraints.

I couldn't move. I couldn't speak properly. I couldn't see. And I couldn't hear. In fact, the only sense that seemed to be working properly was my sense of touch, for even my tongue couldn't taste much aside from the bitter flavor of unconsciousness that currently enveloped it.

"Savannah, listen to me," the voice continued with just the slightest tremble. "You just had a massive panic attack. The doctor said you will be fine, don't worry, but I wanted you to know what was happening. Do you remember?"

That was about the only thing I *did* remember clearly. An onslaught of panic, caused by a bully's death. The more I thought about it, the more it didn't make sense. After all, why would the death of someone I hated spur that much panic, enough to make me go to the infirmary?

I had my answer even before I asked myself the entire question. It wasn't about *who* had died so much as it was the circumstances surrounding her death. I had just seen her, alive and well, merely two days ago at the archery competition. And now, her remains would lie underground for all eternity. And perhaps if I had gone hunting the last two nights like I was supposed to instead of fixating on Callum, I would've caught the beast before this happened.

But instead, I had been so convinced he had been responsible for the deaths that I refused to see reason. After all, it wasn't everyday someone witnessed a big, hulking wolf turn into a boy.

Provided, I didn't actually *see* the transformation, but I was able to piece enough pieces together to know that was what happened.

A warm hand caressed my forehead and down the side of my face. I knew that touch, and it was as comforting as it was graceful. It was a touch that would only belong to my mother, a touch meant to calm and soothe even the most strained individuals.

Though I supposed I fit in that category now, having had a massive panic attack and near-fainting experience in front of the whole town. No one would be talking about my archery feats in the days to come. Instead, they would be talking about the pitiful girl who couldn't keep her emotions in check.

Just like how I was when my brother first passed, only this time, it was worse. This time, it was for a girl I didn't even consider an acquaintance. A girl who had stomped on more people than I cared to admit.

"Sleep, Savannah," my mother cooed, her voice growing more and more focused. "You had a tiring morning, and it will do you some good."

Sleep was the last thing I wanted to do, since I had slept the entire night, but my body had other ideas. It craved the soothing caresses of my mother's fingertips as it slowly grew heavier.

I didn't know how long I was asleep, but when I woke, it was well into the night, and I was alone. And for a heart-stopping minute, all I could think about was Callum, how he was still tied up in my attic despite the fact last night proved his innocence.

All of my senses had returned in full force, and no longer did I feel the least bit tired. I checked myself out before leaving the infirmary, walking home to the sound of crickets.

No longer was I Savannah, the screw-up. By the end of this, I would be known as Savannah, the savior of Ebonrowe.

And the first thing I would do would be to set Callum free and utilize his offered help.

TEN

CALLUM

I was hungry.

No, not hungry—*ravenous*. I was so hungry, I could eat an entire horse and not feel the least bit full. And not once had Savannah returned all day to feed me.

It was like she had vanished, though I knew her better than that. She wouldn't just up and leave, ditching everyone she'd sworn to help. I wouldn't put it past her, however, to starve me.

My stomach gurgled for the one-hundred-millionth time, and I stared daggers at my torso. "Shut up, stomach! We'll be fed soon!"

But no matter how many times I promised my stomach a nice, juicy rabbit, Savannah never came. And I hated to admit I was starting to grow worried, and not *just* because I was currently starving.

Savannah had left early this morning before I had even woken up. I felt the absence of her warmth before I saw not a blonde head in sight. It wasn't long after that that my stomach started yelling at me to feed it, and the rest of the day was spent waiting for her return.

By noon, even my water had run out, which only added to my crappy day.

You could always bust out of your chains, my wolf taunted. *Let me take over, and I'll show her not to mess with us.*

No! I snapped, because despite everything, I still had something I needed to prove to Savannah, and not busting out of her makeshift restraints would help with that. I needed her to believe me, but more than that, I just *needed* her.

My wolf snickered. *Your loss.* And then, he sank further into my subconscious like the most obedient wolf in the world. Which he wasn't.

Great, I thought. *Now, I'm having conversations inside my head with my wolf like a crazy person.*

It was official. This day totally *sucked.*

The sun started setting behind the mountains in the distance, and by the time night finally came, I had all but given up hope that I would see Savannah today.

I had also given up hope that I would be fed as well, but

that was an entirely new dilemma I wasn't ready to entertain just yet. *How will I survive until tomorrow?*

Apparently, I didn't have to think about that, for in the next few seconds, the attic door banged open, and a disheveled Savannah stuck her head in the opening.

I was so taken aback by her appearance, I didn't notice when she came close, so close I could feel her warm breath fan across my cheeks. I didn't even realize she hadn't come bearing gifts of food until she was practically on top of me, reaching behind my back for the leather straps that bound my wrists.

"Today's your lucky day!" she breathed. And then, she undid the bindings, letting them fall to the floor.

With my wrists finally freed, I brought my hands up to my face, inspecting the pink flesh the bindings had entrapped. Aside from a little redness, my wrists were completely fine.

Savannah pushed herself lower to my ankles and started fiddling with the bindings there. Within a beat, they too fell away, and then, she was on me again, reaching around to the back of my neck, feeling along for the knot in the leash. After a few seconds, she yanked it away, tossing it to the side, before scooting back and just staring at me.

I stared back, meeting her gaze for the first time as a free wolf.

She blinked.

I blinked back.

She smiled.

I smiled back.

She pulled her lips into a frown. "Are you copying me?"

I merely chuckled. "Maybe."

"Well, stop it!"

But I didn't want to stop. Instead, I wanted more. More of her touch, more of her scent, more of *her*.

My wolf whined inside my head. It seemed even *he* could sense this stupid fated mate bond thingy.

"You're free now," Savannah said. "Whatcha gonna do about it?"

"Kiss you," I said nonchalantly, my grin only widening in tune to her eyes.

"Unless you want me to slap you, I suggest—"

She never got to finish her sentence, her lips parting with ease as I slowly molded mine over her mouth. The kiss was gentle at first before increasing in intensity as the bond blanketed us in a stream of never-ending passion.

I pulled her closer to me, sucking, nibbling on her lower lip as a moan escaped her throat. And she responded in kind, arching her back as her hands trailed up my torso.

Not once did she slap me, even though she had threatened. It seemed as though she felt the pull as much as I did.

I didn't know if that was a good thing or a bad thing. All I knew was that I couldn't get enough of her. She tasted sweet, like the apples her hair smelled like. And as her tongue darted into my mouth, lightly caressing my own tongue, my head nearly spun as an array of sensations washed over me.

Savannah was kissing me back. *Savannah Collins was actually kissing me back!* A stream of fireworks went off in my head at this realization. The girl Alonsia blessed me with for a mate was actually kissing me back, and not a sweet kiss either, but a ferocious, hungry one that threatened to drown us all in endless passion.

She pulled away just then, a feral smile swiping across her lips. And then, she did the unthinkable.

She slapped me.

Hand made contact with cheek, the sound reverberating throughout my skull along with the pain, as she did, relishing in the cry of shock that escaped my lips. I staggered back an inch, staring at her with widened eyes. I was in utter disbelief.

Her grin widened. "Well, I *did* promise I'd slap you, so…" With a flash of teeth, she closed the gap between us, tenderly touching the spot she had just slapped. "You have a little red hand print *riiiiiight* here."

"Gee, I wonder why," I grumbled before smiling in return. Savannah was a woman who kept her word, and I respected that.

As long as she didn't make slapping me a habit.

Just then, my stomach chose that exact moment to growl once more, breaking the spell the two of us found ourselves under. Savannah's eyes dipped downwards, and one of her eyebrows rose in curiosity.

"Hungry," I said, to which she nodded in

understanding.

"I'm sorry," she said, her voice sounding so sincere I was instantly thrown for a loop.

"Where were you?" I questioned, and the look that crossed her face was so forlorn, I wanted to reach out and hug her.

"I had an…incident."

Incident wasn't very descriptive. It could mean a wide variety of things, ranging in intensity from a light scratch to a sizeable boulder crashing through the window of hope.

She pursed her lips together, and this close, I could see the slight tremble her bottom lip made as it pulled over her top one. It was the latter, it seemed, though in this case, the boulder did more than crash through a measly window.

"Someone else was killed." She said it so casually, so matter-of-factly, that if I wasn't this close to her, I would've completely missed how much this ate at her. "Five in total, but one of the people…"

Her words may have trailed away, but I was able to piece together what she *didn't* say. She knew one of the victims. It was written clear as day on her face. "Was it a family member?"

"No."

"A friend?"

She sucked in a deep breath. "Also no."

At this point, I was at a loss. After all, if it wasn't the first two, how could a death affect her this badly? "An…*acquaintance?*"

In that moment, Savannah speared me with an annoyed look. "She wasn't anyone I liked, alright? That's not what's important here. What's important is the fact she *died*, killed the exact same way as my brother, and—" She immediately cut herself off, her eyes going wide, as if she had said something she wasn't supposed to say.

But now, realization was dawning inside my head, and suddenly, everything began to make sense. Why she had been so aggressive in the beginning, and why she had flip-flopped between hot and cold during these last couple of days. This monster, whatever it was, *had* taken someone from her, someone who meant a lot to her.

Savannah's shoulders sagged as tears blossomed in her eyes. Defeat was etched into her expression so plainly, I wanted to reach out and offer the slightest bit of comfort. "He was only twelve," she said so softly, I didn't know if she was talking to me or herself. "He went out that night, and I didn't stop him."

A big, fat tear chose that moment to roll down her cheek, and with quick reflexes, I reached out and caught it with my finger. "Savannah…" I began, but I didn't know what to say *beyond* that. Everything I could've said sounded so trivial when faced with what she was going through. And it was then when I realized something.

I couldn't offer her comfort, at least not in the way she craved, especially since she had been warring with herself for days on whether or not *I* was the one who had killed her brother. But I *could* offer her something else, something I had already offered before, because mate bond aside and despite everything, I cared about her.

Savannah wiped her eyes with the back of her sleeve, another look coming over her, replacing her sadness. A look of stone. "It doesn't matter anyway," she said. "It's done. You're free. You can go back to your pack or whatever."

But I didn't *want* to go back to my pack, especially not now, while my mate was so distraught and vulnerable. "I meant what I said," I began. "I want to help you."

Savannah blinked, disbelieving. "Why? After everything I've done?"

Because you're my mate, my wolf chimed inside my head, but I knew I couldn't say that to her. She had *just* been introduced to the world of shifters, and I didn't want to scare her off before I figured out the best way to break it to her. "Because though this…thing…is not from my pack, that doesn't mean it's not from some other pack. Or a rogue. Or a different shifter altogether."

Savannah scrunched her face. "Different shifter?"

"There are more than just wolf shifters on the planet," I explained. "There are tiger shifters, hawk shifters, lion shifters, phoenix shifters, dragon shifters…any kind of animal you name can have a shifter counterpart."

"Ant shifters?" Savannah beamed, fighting to hold back a chuckle.

I laughed right along with her. "Yes, I suppose those could exist too." I paused. "Don't underestimate ants, though. They're vicious little pests."

Savannah's laugh was contagious, infecting every inch of the small space. "Phoenixes and dragons aren't real though. They're mythological creatures."

"Oh, they're real," I said. "They're just good at hiding their existence from the world, the only kinds of shifters that do *not* have a non-shifter counterpart."

Savannah furrowed her eyebrows in confusion. "Meaning?"

"Meaning not every wolf you come across is a shifter," I explained. "Every dragon or phoenix or even griffin, however, is."

In fact, mythological creatures were the only kinds of shifters who *shared* a goddess, the only one who wanted her species to have an extra amount of oomph. Quintessa.

Savannah shivered. "Is there anything that does *not* have a shifter counterpart?"

I had thought about that before, but I honestly didn't know. "Single-cells probably don't," I answered honestly. "Plants, bacteria, fungi...things like that probably don't either."

I could tell Savannah's head was spinning, could tell her human brain was having trouble processing all I was telling her. "And rogues?"

I sighed. This was probably something Savannah wouldn't *want* to hear, something she would have an even harder time accepting. But if we had any chance of figuring out the kind of creature her village was dealing with, she needed to know all of it. She needed to know the dark parts of my world, the parts not even my *pack* liked talking about.

"Rogues are just that—rogues," I began. "They could encompass anything that deviates from the norm. A wolf without a pack, a bear who attacks others of its species for no reason, a deer with a taste for human flesh—all of these could encompass rogue shifters. Your kind would probably attribute the weird behavior to rabies, but it's more than that. Rogues were born different, and a lot of the time, their odd behavior results from a chemical imbalance in the brain. In most cases, they are harmless, but sometimes…"

I couldn't bring myself to say the words, but it turned out I didn't need to, for in that instant, a lightbulb went off in Savannah's head, and true fear flashed in her eyes. "You're saying we could be the victims of a rogue?"

"I don't know, but it's a possibility we can't ignore," I told her honestly. "I'd need to actually see one of the bodies to know for sure what kind of animal killed them. That would give me a better idea."

Savannah's face paled. "That's not possible."

I sighed. "Savannah…"

"No, you don't understand." Savannah shook her head. "The bodies have probably been cleaned up by now. You're talking about sneaking into the morgue and intruding on the peaceful slumber of our dead!"

I shook my head, exasperated. I feared this would be the case, that we would have to disrupt the dead. The humans were a lot like shifters in that regard in the sense that we *respected* the dead. And what I was suggesting would be the opposite of that.

But this was also the only way I could see for sure what we were up against. The next full moon was less than a month away, and if we had any chance of preventing the inevitable, we needed to move.

"I know it's not ideal, but—" I began, but Savannah put up a hand, stopping me.

"I trust you," she said. And then, her expression twisted into one of resolve and...*was that determination?* "I trust you," she repeated, "and if you're serious about all this, then we need to move. Before the sun comes up."

ELEVEN

SAVANNAH

I've seen Ebonrowe's morgue countless of times, but I've never once set foot inside of it. It was a place only authorized personnel were allowed to enter, the place bodies went while funeral preparations were made. As children, we were told horror stories about the morgue, stories of curious kids venturing inside, only for whatever deities who lived inside to enslave them, never to be heard from again.

Now that I was older, such stories were just that—stories meant to frighten us to stay far away from that place. But it was still a place I never dared to venture inside, because by that point, respect for the dead had been instilled in us that we no longer *needed* the cautionary tales.

But now, I was about to step inside for the first time in my life, and to say I was nervous would've been an understatement. But for the good of the rest of the town, I would, if only so I could stop this continuous, monthly cycle of death and decay.

Or, *near* monthly, considering this month was one of the rare months where we would be blessed with not one, but *two* full moons. A blue moon, in laymen's terms. Twice the amount of death.

One of the moons has already passed, and we only had around four weeks before the next one came.

After grabbing Callum something to eat and some water, we set off across town with only the waning gibbous to light our way. It was just past one in the morning, when nearly everyone was supposed to be asleep, and yet, I couldn't stop my heart from thrashing inside my chest, as if convinced we were going to be caught at any moment.

Our footsteps crunching the dirt beneath us was the only source of sound, the night silent as if even it was in mourning for what happened during its predecessor. Tension threaded its way through my body with each step we took, and my senses were on high alert, any small snap of a twig immediately sending my mind spinning.

Callum snaked his hand towards mine, threading his fingers through my own and giving a comforting squeeze. We still hadn't discussed fully what this strange pull was between us, but with everything going on, we haven't had the chance. I hadn't even known Callum for a week yet, but already, it was like my body was in tune to his against its own volition.

It was unlike anything I had ever experienced before, not even with Trevor. My body physically hurt when it was away from him as if he were a drug I couldn't get enough of.

I was well and truly fucked.

By the time we reached the morgue, my body was absolutely vibrating with pent-up tension, so much so that I instantly felt sick. Callum would never understand how much this place creeped me out, and not just because of the stories I was told as a child.

That dead body I had seen when I was six scarred me in a way nothing else would. That was the day my innocence irrevocably died, and not even my parents could bring back the happy-go-lucky child I was.

They had found out days later that I had snuck out, when I finally broke down and told them. And they didn't even punish me for directly disobeying them, instead pulling me into a group hug and trying to comfort me as best they could. But nothing they did worked, and when my brother died as well, I broke completely, numbness spreading throughout my entire system.

I didn't cry, not like my parents did. Instead, I felt hollow as my mind struggled to keep up with my body breaking down.

"Hey," Callum suddenly said, seeming to have sensed a

change in me. "Hey, Savannah, it's okay. You're okay."

It took me a moment to realize he was directly in front of me, enveloping me in a strong embrace that nearly had me melting. I buried my face into his chest, breathing in his strong scent and willing myself *not* to cry. I'd already done too much of that already.

Instead, I said, "I had a massive panic attack in the square this morning." I felt Callum stiffen as he held me, as I admitted to him something that had never happened to me before. I didn't *get* panic attacks. Instead, I buried everything deep inside myself and hoped it wouldn't fester.

"That's why you didn't come all day today," Callum said matter-of-factly. "What happened?"

"I don't know. I thought every part of me broke when my brother had died, but seeing Matilda meet the same fate…" I hiccupped, and Callum rubbed soothing circles into my back. I sucked in a gasping breath. "A part of me died just a little bit more. Fuck, I didn't even *like* Matilda, and yet—"

"It could've happened to anyone," Callum said solemnly. "It could've happened to your parents."

I sniffed, fighting back tears, because Callum had hit the nail on the dot. "I feel so fucking powerless!"

"No, you're not. That's why we're here," Callum said. "To put a stop to whatever's happening."

I pulled out of his embrace just then, my eyes locking on his warm gaze. "Why are you still here?" I questioned, my voice barely above a whisper. "I practically kidnapped you, tied you up in my attic, and when I finally free you, you're still here."

A soft smile ghosted Callum's lips. "Because I understand why you did it," he said. "And if the roles had been reversed, I would've done the same."

It was something he had told me before, but I didn't realize until then how much his words meant to me. I didn't realize how much I *needed* to hear those words again, that despite all the bad, there was still some good in the world.

A thought suddenly came over me, one itching for an answer. "Callum," I began, to which he hummed in response, "if it turns out the wounds were caused by a wolf, what would you do?"

Callum pursed his lips in thought. "I suppose I'd have to somehow get a message to my father to be on the lookout for a rogue wolf or one from another pack."

"And what if it turns out all this was done by a wolf from *your* pack?"

"It's not," Callum said suddenly, though not defensively. "I would know if it was."

I scoffed. "No, you wouldn't!"

"Savannah." Callum sighed. "Savannah, my dad right now is the alpha, and I'm his successor. Do you know what that means?"

I shook my head, unable to comprehend the bombshell Callum just dropped on me. *Future alpha?* I thought, my eyes going wide. *Holy shit! I kidnapped the son of an alpha!*

"It means," Callum continued, seeming not to have

noticed the new direction my thoughts were taking, "we can sense all of our wolves and tap into their minds if need be. If there was a wolf in our pack with nefarious purposes, we would know, and they would've been dealt with a long time ago."

His words should've brought me a sense of comfort, but all they did was spur on more questions. After all, what he was saying should've been impossible. What he was suggesting was a sense of mind reading, stuff that would've made more sense in one of Trevor's books than in real life.

"We're wasting time," Callum said "I'll explain more about my kind later, if you still want to know. But now, we need to figure out exactly what has been slaughtering your people."

I nodded in agreement, putting my questioning thoughts aside, as we stepped into the morgue. Immediately, the smell of death and decay accosted me, the air plummeting in temperature as what I envisioned were ghosts wrapped around me. I used to think ghosts were fiction, but if werewolves were real...

Callum led me deeper into the morgue, the stench suddenly becoming too overwhelming. I started breathing through my mouth in heavy pants, listening for something, *anything*, other than our footsteps on the cold, hard stone.

"There's no one else here," Callum said, as if that was supposed to reassure me, but all it did was send even more goosebumps down my spine.

"What about ghosts?" I hissed, hating the dark turn my

thoughts were taking.

At this, Callum barked out a laugh. "Someone's been reading way too many ghost stories."

"Okay, first of all, I don't read!" I snapped before realizing how defensive and *untrue* that was. I didn't read for pleasure so much, but I *did* read when I had to. "And second of all, if werewolves are real—"

"We're not werewolves," Callum said defensively. "We're wolf *shifters.*"

"Right, whatever." Perhaps *werewolf* was only a term humans used. I waved my hands around the small space. "Point is, if those exist, who's to say ghosts don't either?"

"They don't," Callum said. Straight and to the point. "The dead don't linger on the plain of the living."

I felt like I had been slapped. "Wait, the plain of the living? Are you suggesting there are different *plains* now?"

"Savannah, focus!" Callum barked. "One thing at a time."

"Right, okay." I forced my shoulders to relax and my mind to stop thinking about everything at once. The last thing I needed was another panic attack in a place where I was surrounded by dead people.

We walked a bit more in silence, scanning every inch of the morgue for any sign of animal wounds. There were bodies of varying ages littering the morgue, from elderly to infants who didn't make it to their first year. All of them, dead of natural causes and illnesses.

Not one of them bore the deep marks a victim of the

beast should sport, and with each body we passed, my uneasiness grew.

Until Callum suddenly stopped, causing me to almost collide with his back. "Is this one of them?" he asked suddenly, staring at something directly in front of him.

At the body of one of the victims from this morning.

It wasn't Matilda Brant, thank fuck, because after this morning, I didn't think I could bear to see her mutilated body again. But seeing the deep, animalistic wounds carved into flesh still spurred something within me, and I couldn't manage more than a small nod.

Callum glanced at me, took one look at my frozen expression, and nodded in understanding. "Cover your eyes, Savannah," he said, turning back towards the corpse. "I promise to be quick."

I did as he ordered, and soon, the world went dark as I shut my eyes as tightly as I could, bringing my hands to cover them further. I heard more footsteps as Callum moved towards the corpse, heard the sound of a sheet rustling as he pulled it back to get a better look.

A gasp ripped its way out of me as silence encompassed the small space, the only comfort the fact that Callum was only a few paces away. And somehow, I knew that he wouldn't let anything happen to me.

I pictured Callum running his hands along the seams of the wounds, sniffing around the way wolves often did. I zoned in on his breathing as he studied the lacerations, could practically hear the gears turning in his head as he assessed the wounds.

And then, he replaced the sheet and shuffled back until he was directly in front of me, shielding me from the gruesome scene.

I opened my eyes and tore my hands away, and the first thing I saw was his grim expression.

"They're wolf marks," he said solemnly, and I felt my world shatter just a little bit more. "You could be dealing with a rogue, or worse, a foreign pack."

~*~

I felt like I was floating, jumping from one cloud to the next, untethered to my earthly body as I drifted farther and farther away. I was no longer in control of my movements, instead allowing something else to take the wheel, promising to take me far away from the pain I had known.

I didn't remember the journey back to my house, my eyes unseeing as clouds morphed back into white walls and a white ceiling and a window and a door. Soft covers enveloped me in an even softer bed, and I sighed as my muscles loosened one at a time.

My bed dipped, and I was surprised to see Callum on the edge, always a silent beacon of light. "You're awake," he noted, seeming to sag in relief.

I shook my head. "What happened?"

"I don't know," Callum said honestly. "One moment, you were with me, and the next, I felt like I was dragging a corpse. You've been like that for a good hour."

I shuddered as memories accosted my subconscious. The morgue, the body with animalistic lacerations, and then, Callum's voice as he told me what he believed I was dealing with. Then, nothing as my mind went blank, my soul floating high in the sky while my body was left to shoulder the burden of my village's curse.

"I'm sorry," I said quietly, because I didn't know what else to say.

"Don't be. You just had a bit of a shock," Callum said. "I'm going to send word to my father tomorrow. He needs to know what's been happening here."

The bed dipped again as he made to get up, but my arm shot out, clutching his before he could make his escape. "Stay," I said, my voice hoarse. "Please. I don't want to be alone tonight."

Callum stared at me for a few seconds before relenting, scooting himself further up the bed, hands pulling me closer to him as he slid underneath the covers.

His chin rested atop my head, breath fanning across my scalp, and for a moment, I felt safe as my body melted into him, my heart beating in tune to his.

"Sleep, Savannah," he said, the vibration of his voice sending me further into relaxation.

Without having to be told twice, I did.

TWELVE

CALLUM

I didn't know if I could telecommunicate with my dad from this far away, but I had to try. The only other option would be to leave, and I couldn't do that to Savannah, not after last night.

So, in the wee hours of the morning, as Savannah slumbered peacefully in my arms, I strained towards my father's mind, surprised when I felt the connection, tugging on it so my father would know I was there.

Callum? my father said, his voice groggy as if I had woken him up. *Son, is that you?*

I nearly wept at the sound of his voice, even if it was

only in my mind. I didn't realize until now how much I missed him, how much I missed all of the pack, but especially him. He may have been a hard-ass, but he loved me, and I didn't know what I would do without his guidance. *Yes, it's me*, I said, and I nearly felt the relief that flowed through the bond as I said those words.

Where are you? my father asked. *When Sammy told us what happened, we went to search for you, but after finding nothing, we wrote you off as dead!*

I'm in Ebonrowe. Long story, I said.

Relief soon turned to anger as my father roared down the bond, *What the hell are you doing there?*

I flinched. My father was scary when he was angry, even if his anger wasn't directed at me. I couldn't very well tell him the truth, that a human girl practically kidnapped me because she thought I was the one responsible for her people's deaths, but I didn't know what else to do. If I told him the truth, he would hunt Savannah down, and I couldn't let that happen.

So, I opted to tell him a variation of the truth. *I found my mate.*

Something akin to wonder flowed down the bond before being replaced by skeptical cynicism. *Your mate...is in Ebonrowe?*

Yes, I said. *I know how crazy this sounds, but—*

No wolf lives in Ebonrowe! It's a human village!

I know, but—

There hasn't been a wolf-human pairing in centuries, not

since Alonsia cut them off from us! my father thundered. *This isn't possible!*

Soon, I was angry. The mate bond was something we didn't know until we experienced it ourselves, and I was *sure* that was what I was experiencing with Savannah. Alonsia or not, it was ignorant to believe nothing was going on between us. *It's true, Dad!* I protested. *Savannah is—*

It was in that instance that I realized I made a mistake. Anger like I had never felt before thundered down the bond, nearly rattling me to my core. And then, nothing as my father's steely resolve washed over me. Very rarely had he ever exercised his scary alpha power over me, but he was doing it now, and even though he was miles away, my wolf begged me to run from his wrath. Actually *whined*, and my wolf wasn't a whiner.

My father's cold voice slithered through the bond again, sending a shiver down my spine. *The human's name is Savannah,* he said. *How could you be so stupid?*

Believe me or don't! I roared, now beyond furious. I would die before I let my father take Savannah from me. *That's the least of our worries!*

Silence. Then:

What the hell are you talking about?

I sighed, gearing myself up to drop the biggest bombshell on my father I ever had. *There's a foreign wolf in our lands. I don't know if it's a rogue or a member of a different pack, but it's killing off the people of this village.*

Shock ran down the bond as my father took all this in.

Impossible, he said. *There isn't another pack for miles!*

I know what I saw! I protested. *The wounds are wolf-caused! Just…be on the lookout, please!*

Because if there *was* a foreign wolf on our lands, then we had bigger problems. We were in danger too.

Okay, my father finally conceded. *When are you coming home?*

Not until I see this through, I said. *I'll be in touch.* And then, I abruptly severed the connection before my father could say anything else. Before he could use his power as alpha to order me back, because he was the only one who could.

Savannah stirred in my arms just then, bringing me back to her, to the way she fit perfectly against me, to the way she breathed as she slept.

Mate, my wolf chimed, itching to formally claim her and make her mine. I pulled on the reins as hard as I could before doing something we'd regret later. Humans weren't like shifters. Their relationships tended to blossom overtime, whereas ours were more like a freight train of feelings that threatened to devour us.

She probably had no idea what she was experiencing, and I wasn't ready to tell her for fear of scaring her away. Rejection was a fickle thing, and to be rejected by her would be akin to losing a limb.

Worse than that, my wolf chimed, and I had to agree. It would feel like dying, both my soul and my heart shredding in two until I was left with…nothing. Just an empty husk where I was just existing, unable to feel the slightest bit of emotion.

Losing her would break me in more ways than one.

Just like losing her brother had broken her, a taunting voice whispered deep within my subconscious, one that differed from my wolf. I tensed, because in a way, that was true. Savannah was a broken soul, molded into a feral thing capable of shooting the first damn wolf she came across. Something told me she would've turned out a lot differently, would've been happier, if she wasn't haunted by her village's beast.

"The first time I saw a dead body, I was just six years old," Savannah suddenly spoke, jolting me out of my thoughts.

I jumped, because all this time, I thought she was asleep. *When did she wake up?*

Savannah sucked in a deep breath, her body trembling with the memory. "My parents told Mathias and I to not go outside when the alarms sounded month after month, full moon after full moon." She paused, cocking her head so she could stare at me over her shoulder. "But one day, my curiosity got the best of me, and for the first time, I disobeyed my parents."

I didn't know what to say, the only thought going through my mind the fact I now had her brother's name. *Mathias.* My grip on her tightened, as if my hold alone would be enough to shield her from such painful memories.

"The victim had been Mrs. Harlow, the village baker at

the time. I had *just* seen her not even twenty-four hours before, and there she was in the center of the square with the same damn lacerations you saw last night! Dead!" She shuddered, shifting her body to face me. "I had to lie to him about what I saw, my own *brother*, whom I never lied to in my life!"

"Oh, Savannah," I said on a sigh. "No one should have to go through that."

"Oh, it gets worse." She let out a bitter chuckle. "The night before Mathias's twelfth birthday, he snuck out with some friends. I caught him in the act, but instead of ordering him back or raising the alarm, I told him to have fun." Tears glistened in her eyes as she recanted her story. "He…he never made it home."

"That wasn't your fault," I said, because it was the truth. "You couldn't have known."

"Should I've?" Savannah shook her head. "There was a full moon that night. I should've stopped him, but I didn't, because his birthday was the next day! The next damn day! I was only *fourteen*!"

"Exactly," I said, as if it should've been obvious. "You were *only* fourteen."

"I should've stopped him," Savannah whispered, though whether she was still talking to me or to herself, I didn't know. And then, she buried her face into my chest, her body wracked with sobs. "And then, you come along, and despite the fact I almost *killed* you, you decide to stick around. Why, Callum? Why, when you should've hated me?"

"I could never hate you," I said, and it was the truth. I was angry, yes, but I understood. Plus, the mate bond made it physically impossible to hate her.

"But you should," Savannah said. "I'm so many shades of fucked-up, you wouldn't be able to tell which is which."

I let out a soft chuckle, feeling the rumble deep in my chest. "I never had much of a childhood either," I admitted. "Being groomed to take on the alpha position from an early age didn't give me much time to, you know…be a kid."

Plus, even though I knew my father loved me, he was such a hard-ass, as if he forgot to turn off his position as alpha at times in order to just…be my dad.

"I'm sorry," Savannah said. "Being forced to grow up before your time is the absolute worst."

"Agreed!" A brief smile appeared on my lips before vanishing with one more sobering thought. "I contacted my father about the foreign wolf."

This seemed to perk Savannah up. "And?"

"He wasn't aware of any trespassers, but he'll keep an eye out."

Savannah pulled her lips into a frown. "Trespassers?"

I nodded. "Though not technically a part of pack lands, your village still borders us. Any foreign wolf who comes should be of immediate concern for us."

Savannah nodded in understanding. "What happens now?"

"Now, we wait," I said honestly. My father would

contact me if he finds anything.

Seeming to accept that answer, Savannah relaxed her shoulders and closed her eyes, and for hours, we stayed in that position. For hours, I allowed myself to be the comfort she needed, the escape she desperately craved.

And for now, that was enough.

~*~

Days passed by in a blur, where I was mostly confined to the attic. Since Savannah's parents still had no idea she was harboring a boy in their home, I was only allowed to come out during the days they worked and some of the nights. Savannah, however, was practically glued to my side, even taking her meals to the attic, where we would sit and talk for hours.

She told me about her archery competition, where she had scored second place. And I told her of pack life. She seemed especially enraptured when I explained our hierarchy and how each wolf had a place within the pack.

"Just like actual wolves," she chimed, flopping onto her back.

I chuckled. "I mean, wolf is in the name, so..." And then, she laughed as well, and soon, we were two balls of laughter without any sign of stopping.

Noise filled the small space of the attic as our chests heaved in perfect sync, heat unfurrowing in my lower gut as I watched her match my tone. And soon, her eyes locked onto mine as she burrowed into my soul.

The laughter slowly died down.

And confusion marred her features as she asked, "You feel it too, don't you?"

I didn't have to ask to know what she meant. The mate bond, the thing that had been plaguing us since day one.

I slowly nodded, letting my silence speak for me.

Savannah let out a heavy sigh. "But why? I've never felt this with anybody else."

The answer was on the tip of my tongue, but I couldn't bring myself to tell her. At least not yet. But I also didn't want to lie to her, so I said nothing once again.

Thankfully, she let the subject drop, but as we returned to our laughter, I couldn't help the pang I felt in my gut. At some point, I would have to tell her.

But now was not the time.

THIRTEEN

SAVANNAH

Callum was hiding something. I was sure of it. The glistening sweat on his brow and the way his eyes shifted ever so slightly, just short of widening, were telltale signs that he wasn't being one hundred percent truthful.

Of course, he didn't outright lie either, but he might as well have with the way he kept silent. And that stung just as much as any lie had.

I scooted back, throwing some much-needed distance between us as I tried to tell my wounded heart this was just a bump in the road, that he wasn't deliberately trying to hurt me. He *held* me, for crying out loud, and I unshed every single trauma I held onto.

Besides, we had only known each other a little over a week, tied together due to our mutual want of bringing the beast down. Me because of what it had done to my brother, and Callum because a foreign wolf was dangerous. We had only barely just started getting to know each other, and yet, it was as if my entire body was fighting with my brain.

My brain was the more reasonable one, reluctant to rush into something with somebody we barely knew. But my body continuously hummed his name, a vibration growing deep within my core. And my body was winning.

"Did your father find anything yet?" I inquired, if only so it would distract from the want pooling between my legs. I wasn't an overtly sexual person, so this was...unusual for me, as if my body for once wasn't my own.

Callum frowned. "Not yet." He paused, a furrow creasing between his brows as if he had more to say but didn't know how else to say it. Eventually, he decided to just let it out. "He hasn't been able to sense a foreign wolf, and neither have the other wolves."

I sagged. This news was deeply upsetting, because it meant we were back to square one. "Is he sure the wolf isn't just, you know...masking his scent?"

Callum blinked at me as if I had just asked a really stupid question. "Wolves can't mask scents. At least not without the assistance of a very powerful witch, and there isn't a witch coven for miles." He shook his head. "Plus, witches by and large stay out of human affairs. No witch would grant a wolf the ability to mask its scent with the purpose of killing humans."

My head was spinning, and it was taking everything in me to not lose it. "Witches exist too?" I practically screamed in his face, on the verge of hyperventilating.

Callum nodded solemnly, regretfully. "They were born in sync with shifters," he explained. "And they mostly keep to themselves, living in seclusion on some of the highest peaks in the world."

"Not. Helping," I seethed, my panic like its own untamed beast, running rampant throughout my veins and effectively chasing away the heat I felt earlier. I couldn't breathe, my heart threatening to burst out of my chest, as dizziness began to take hold.

And all I could think was, *Please, god, not again!*

But then, right before I crashed to the ground, strong arms bounded around me, propping me up against an even stronger chest. "I've got you," Callum murmured against my hair. "I need you to breathe, okay?"

I managed to nod my head, fighting to suck in a breath of air, but it was hard, so damn hard. My chest ached, my lungs, everywhere *burned*, scorching me from the inside out as I fought not to drown under my panic's crushing weight.

"Breathe with me," Callum said, rocking me back and forth as he took slow, deep breaths.

"I can't!" I wailed, fighting against him as spots danced along my vision.

"Yes," Callum said in that same calm tone, "you can."

And I didn't know if it was because of his reassurances, his belief in me, that led me away from the edge, but as I tried to match his breaths, the panic started to subside. No longer was I floundering, waiting for the inevitable to pull me under. Instead, I was floating, held up by an invisible raft, as the currents finally calmed down.

"I'm going to let go now," Callum said the moment I stopped thrashing in his arms. And then, he let go.

I waited for another bomb to detonate, another curveball aimed directly at my head to finally make contact. But instead, I felt...nothing. It wasn't peace I felt; that would've felt too kind, like floating on the fluffiest cloud.

No, it wasn't peace that now flooded my body but resignation. I've already had two panic attacks, the only two I've ever had in my eighteen years of living. And the common denominator, it seemed, was Callum.

He stared at me, worry creasing his brows, but I couldn't manage anything other than a swift nod. Because for the time being, I *was* fine, even though I wasn't *fine*.

"What are you thinking?" he questioned, reluctant. As if not quite ready to hear the answer.

There was a lot I wanted to say to him. I wanted to tell him that all this was too much. A little over a week ago, I was still convinced the creature that killed every full moon was a normal, bloodthirsty animal, like a bear or even a tiger. And now, I was launched into a world fraught with things I only ever considered fiction.

And that wasn't even counting the strange attraction to a boy I hadn't known that long. I wasn't naive enough to believe that what I was experiencing was love, because stuff like love at first sight was only the stuff of fairytales and children's stories. *Lust perhaps?* But that didn't sound quite right either, especially considering I've never experienced sexual attraction of this magnitude before.

But I didn't know if I could reveal any of that to him. After all, what spurred me into a panic was what he grew up with. This was his entire world, and who was I to start questioning it?

So, I lied. "Nothing."

"Savannah…" Callum began, his voice sending a shiver down my spine. It was the tone he used when he knew I wasn't being entirely truthful.

"Can we change the subject please?" I pleaded. "I don't want to talk about this anymore."

Callum ignored my plea, inching closer to my broken form. "I get it. It seems like everything you thought you knew was one big lie, and as more gets revealed, you feel even more overwhelmed." He paused, thoughtful. "But, Savannah, you're as much a part of this world now—"

"I never *asked* to be a part of this world!" I snapped, causing him to flinch.

Callum stretched out his spine and continued, "Regardless of whether or not you asked for it is irrelevant." His words sliced like a knife down to my core. "Humans used to know about us, about witches, all of it, a very long time ago."

This caught my attention. "What...happened?" I asked tentatively, unsure if I wanted to know the answer.

Callum sucked in a deep breath. "They started enslaving us, experimenting on us, the like...and as such, their knowledge of our kind was erased. They were punished—brutally—and then stripped of their memories, and to this day, we have lived separate lives," he explained. "Each shifter species has its own goddess, as do the witches, and it was through their command that humans lost the biggest gift they have ever been given."

"Until now," I said bitterly, my anger flaring up at the thought of what my ancestors had put Callum's people through. No one had a right to be kept in captivity and tortured, and yet, that was exactly what humans did. As if we were the superior beings.

As if we owned them.

"You're not at fault for the actions of others centuries ago," Callum said sternly. "I need you to know that."

"I *do* know that!" I spat. It was the truth. This had happened centuries ago, and I was only one person. But that realization did not erase the guilt I felt in my gut.

Callum nodded. "That was also the first and only time the witches ever got involved in human affairs." He laughed bitterly. "They aided the goddesses in punishing the humans. Can you imagine? The normally neutral witches set on a path of pure destruction."

"I'm sorry," I said, not knowing what else to say. It was all too horrible to imagine, but I couldn't deny my ancestors deserved whatever hell was unleashed on them.

"Don't be. The past is the past." Callum shrugged. "All we can hope for now is a better future."

"You don't think humans could eventually earn forgiveness and be given the knowledge again, do you?" I inquired. A world where everyone knew everything there was to know meant a world devoid of secrets and free of fear.

Fear of the unknown was a powerful tool, and I had been living in its shadow all my life.

"I don't know," Callum said, "but I suppose we're about to find out."

This sparked my curiosity. "What do you mean?"

Callum opened his mouth. Closed it. Then opened it again. "You know, and for some reason, Alonsia hasn't struck us down yet." He paused cryptically. "You could be the test, the first human in centuries allowed knowledge of our kind."

A shiver snaked down my spine. Being the only human allowed this information was a huge responsibility, and I didn't know how I felt about that. "Who's Alonsia?"

"She's the wolf shifter goddess," Callum explained. "Sister to the witch goddess, Hectora, and only one of the many shifter goddesses."

"Goddess," I repeated, testing the word out myself. "As in female?"

Callum nodded slowly. "It is said Alonsia gave birth to our kind centuries ago, and for that, we owe everything to her," he clarified. "My father may be the alpha of my pack now, and later, me, but you will find shifter and witch society are largely matriarchal, *especially* witch society."

My village was split fifty-fifty, but I've heard of other human settlements adopting a patriarchal structure. Even our gods—something I wasn't sure I believed in—were predominantly male, so to hear that the opposite was true for the supernatural races...

"We believe fertility and the emotional graces of a woman are the strongest," Callum continued, "because without them, we would cease to exist."

I scoffed. "Some human settlements may disagree with you."

Callum pulled his lips into a frown, his eyes raking over me as if trying to find some hidden hurt. They were pitiful eyes, eyes born of melancholy resignation. I simply shrugged, because it wasn't a big deal to me.

We were born of two different cultures, two different world spaces. And I was strangely okay with that.

The rest of the day passed by in a blur, and soon, the sun had disappeared completely. But we were still together, still talking about anything and everything, every single little detail about our lives in order to pass the time.

It had been a long time since I had someone to talk to with this level of carefree abandonment, someone I didn't hold back with. The only other person I had this level of intimacy with was Trevor, and those days have long passed, especially since he still hadn't gotten over *us*.

With Trevor, there was an expectation, like a trade. He would be my shoulder to cry on, listen to my ramblings, and take those to mean I was willing to give us another shot. He wasn't a guy who thought he owned me, per se, but that expectation was still there.

But with Callum, there was none of that. Despite the weird attraction I had towards him, we were just two strangers trying to find our place in the world. Two strangers bound by a cruel sense of fate with only ourselves to keep each other company.

I didn't remember when I had fallen asleep, but when I woke, we were snuggled up against each other on the cold, hard floor. Fur tickled my nose as I rolled over, surprised to see he had at some point shifted during the middle of the night. I was curled up in a bed of fluffiness, my body strangely warm despite the chill in the air.

He was still asleep, but when I ran my fingers through his fur ever so slightly, the muscles in his torso twitched involuntarily. And for some reason, that brought a smile to my face as I played with the tiny white hairs.

It was then when I realized I was feeling something I hadn't felt in a long time.

Content.

FOURTEEN

CALLUM

The slightest brush of fingertips stirred me awake, causing my muscles to tense and an involuntary shiver to wrack my spine. I woke with a start, eyes flying open with the unexpected touch as I scanned my surroundings.

Sometime during the night, I had shifted for the first time in over a week as a means of keeping the cold out of my bones. My fur kept me warm through the harshest of Ebonrowe's wintery air, but there was another ball of warmth curled into my side, one that wasn't a part of me.

Savannah, my human side whispered with realization, and my wolf half had to agree. The little bundle of warmth tucked comfortably against my side was Savannah Collins, the only human who I allowed to get close to me. She was already awake, eyes locked on her fingertips as they played with my fur, drawing random shapes along my skin. My wolf let out a howl, overjoyed at the prospect that our fated mate was this close to us, touching us with such careful caresses, but I reigned him in, trying to keep him in check. Because the last thing I wanted was to scare her off with too much affection.

Savannah didn't seem to mind, however, as she continuously ran her fingers through my fur, a half-smile on her face. *Good morning, Sunshine,* I spoke, directing my thoughts to her.

I had absolutely no idea if I would be able to communicate with her in this way. After all, she wasn't a wolf shifter, so I had no idea if her human brain could even *handle* telepathic communication. But when she jolted, eyes locking onto mine, I could tell she *had* heard me plain as day.

And she was startled by it. My own mate was startled that I could communicate with her through our minds while in this form.

"What just happened?" she questioned, her fingers stilling, as she stared at me in confusion. "Did you…did you just…?"

I gave her a single nod, enough to ensure her she wasn't just hearing things. *While in this form, I can use my mind to communicate.*

"How is this possible?" she wondered. "I'm not like you."

A part of me thought it had something to do with the bond, but another part of me disregarded that idea. After all, we hadn't solidified it, so the bond was nowhere near as strong as it could be. *I don't know,* I admitted. *To be honest, I wasn't sure if this would work.*

"Well, it does." Savannah scrunched her face. And then, her face brightened as if an idea came to her. "You said humans used to know about you, right?"

Yes, I said.

"You probably could've communicated with humans in this manner all along!" she chirped, a smirk curving her lips until a frown enveloped it. "Unless that was one more thing your goddesses took from my people."

It's possible, I admitted. It was the only other thing that made sense. Even if Alonsia and the others had taken that ability away from the humans, if Savannah were in fact a test...

I shook my head. My brain hurt. I wasn't used to thinking on such a deep level, but it seemed Savannah *was* a deep thinker.

My wolf nudged me forward, urging me to claim her as mine, but I refrained. *No!* I scolded him. *She doesn't know yet!*

"Doesn't know what yet?"

At that moment, I froze. *Crap!* I seethed. I hadn't meant to project that last thought out to her, but apparently, I did, and now, she was staring at me as if I had sprouted two heads.

She let out a bitter laugh. "I knew you were hiding something!"

Once again, my wolf urged me to claim her, but with unprecedented strength, I was able to keep him at bay. I wasn't used to being able to control him so effortlessly.

Perhaps he was finally starting to listen to me.

The human in me sighed. *This isn't a conversation I think we should have while I'm in this form.* And then, I shifted back, and her eyes bugged out as she finally witnessed the shift for the first time.

"Huh. So, that's how it works," she said, her eyes dipping lower, swaying to my junk. A blush coated her cheeks. "What happened to the clothes I gave you?"

"I took them off," I explained, pointing to the bundling heap in the corner of the attic. "I didn't think you'd be happy if I shredded through them."

Savannah shook her head and blinked. "Right…well…you can put them on again now."

For a moment, I was confused, until I finally felt what had her in a knot. My lower half ached, swelling up to the size of a baseball bat.

I was unbelievably *hard,* and my mate took quick notice.

She stared at it for several seconds, her lips pursed. "Huh," she said. "So, *that's* what a dick looks like."

Oh my god!

Mortification flooded my veins, but that didn't seem to stop my cock from swelling to a seemingly unnatural size. "You've…you've never seen one before?" Somehow, I found that hard to believe.

Savannah shook her head. "I'm not really much of a sexual person," she explained, shrugging. "If it happens, it happens, but it's not something I *need* to partake in."

I stared at her in disbelief. "So, you're ace?"

She shrugged. "I'm not really sure what I am, but I've never really felt the need."

Interesting, I thought, shoving that piece of information down to revisit later.

"Plus, I'm not really that big on pain," Savannah added. "And *that* looks like it would be enough to split me in half. Like an alien from another world."

Shock slammed into me. "Did you just call my dick an alien?"

"I mean, it's sure twitching like one," Savannah said, soon meeting my eyes. "Can you put it away now please? It's…doing things to me I'm not used to."

I smirked, moving towards my discarded clothes. "You mean…you're aroused?"

"*Yes!*" she seethed. "And I don't like it, so please put it away before someone gets hurt!"

I laughed, quickly slipping into my clothes. "You're probably the first person I've ever met who wants to be *un-aroused*."

Savannah stared at me point-blank. "Come anywhere near me with that thing, and I'll make you wish you were born with a vagina instead."

I flinched. "Noted," I grumbled. *So, cementing the bond is out.* Not that I really *needed* to cement anything with her. Just being with her was enough, but it would've been nice to one day make it official, like how marriage was for humans. "You know, the bulge will still be there."

Savannah looked downright murderous. "Do I need to force you to wear more layers so it's finally covered?"

I shook my head. "No, I'll just...cover it with my hands?"

"I swear, if you force me to watch while you—"

"Not what I meant!" I yelled. "Geez, you make it sound like I'm some sort of sexual animal!"

"Well, you *are* a wolf, so..."

"Newsflash," I said. "Humans are animals too."

"Can we please stop talking about this?" Savannah whined. "You're making my lower half feel even *more* weird."

"It's natural, babe." I laughed. "But fine. Let's talk about the mate bond instead."

If words could freeze over, I was positive we were in a frozen tundra right about now. As if on cue, any lightheartedness that existed between us fizzled out like a dying flame, replaced by curious mortification.

"Mate…bond?" Savannah questioned breathlessly, and for the first time, I saw fear flash in her irises. Savannah was *scared* of the thing that was happening between us, and I didn't know what I could do to reassure her that it was nothing to be scared of.

Seeing her like that nearly broke me, because for once, *I* was on the receiving end of her panic.

"I don't know how it happened," I quickly began, "but I wanted to tell you right. When you were ready and certainly not in *this* setting."

"*This* was what you were keeping from me?" Savannah snarled. "What the hell did you do to me?"

"*I* did nothing to you!" I said. "This is Alonsia's doing, her way of merging two compatible souls together!"

"What *is* it?" Savannah questioned, fear giving way to curiosity.

This was it, the moment I would either keep or lose her. I didn't think my wolf would be able to handle it if I lost her. "We're fated mates, Savannah," I explained softly. "*Soul* mates. The stuff you're feeling, same as what *I'm* feeling, is a direct result of the bond."

Savannah shook her head, baring her teeth. "I knew it!" she practically screamed. "I knew what I was feeling wasn't truly me!"

That, I at least agreed with her on. "It's the bond," I explained. "Usually, it only happens between two shifters, oftentimes in the same species. For it to happen between a shifter and a human is…strange, though I suppose it could've happened during the years your people knew about us."

There. My huge secret was finally out in the open, and for once, it actually felt *good* to unload it all. Because finally, Savannah knew, and now, she had a viable explanation for how she was feeling. I saw relief flood through her at this knowledge, in direct contrast to the panic I was *expecting* her to go through. For a moment, I had high hopes that we'd make it out of this okay.

Until she opened her mouth again. "How do I break it?"

My face fell, my heart feeling like it had been wrenched from my chest. *Stupid!* I scolded myself. After all, with the way everything practically had been forced upon her, I knew my hopes had been unnaturally high. Of course she would want a way out, a means of making her life normal again. *Of course she wouldn't want me in the same way I wanted her.*

My soul practically shattered as I went to answer her. "I don't know, but if that's what you truly want, I'm sure we can—"

"Callum," Savannah began with a cheeky smile on her face. "I'm kidding."

Her words slammed into me, and for a moment, I thought I had misheard her. "You…what?"

"I'm kidding!" she repeated, her smile widening. "Joking, joshing you, not serious, whatever you want to call it."

"I…" I stammered, at a loss for words. *This girl was going to be the death of me.*

Savannah's smile faltered. "Callum…are you okay?"

"Yes, I'm fine," I said, smiling to prove the lie. *Just slowly recovering from nearly having my soul shattered. No big deal.*

"Geez, if I knew my joke would've affected you this much, I would've just kept my mouth shut," Savannah said, scooting closer to me. "I'm sorry."

"Don't be," I said, "but may I ask why?"

"Why what?"

"Why are you so calm?" I pestered. "I just dropped a huge bombshell that I wasn't sure how you would receive."

Savannah shrugged. "It *did* come as a shock at first. I'm not going to lie." She paused. "But it also explains so much, and believe it or not…I don't actually hate it. The sensations are weird, yes, but they're also refreshing, as if I needed a reminder that I was still human, that I was *normal.*"

"There *is* no normal," I argued, surprising her.

"There is when everyone else my age has been losing their virginity left and right when they were sixteen, and here I am, still a virgin, still having no desire to partake in sex." She sighed. "Like I'm something broken."

"There's nothing broken about you, Savannah," I said, meaning every word. "When you're finally ready, you'll know, and if that never comes, that doesn't mean there's something wrong with you. Besides, sex is overrated anyway."

At this, Savannah burst out laughing. "I think you'll find a lot of people disagree with you."

I shrugged. "They don't matter," I said. "Besides, what's there to look forward to? It's painful, messy, unsanitary...not to mention the wide array of diseases that can spawn from it. You're not missing out on much."

"How do you know?" Savannah teased. "Have you ever done it before?"

"Once when I was fifteen," I admitted. I was just coming into myself, and curiosity got the best of me, so I laid with someone two years older. It was a literal shitshow, as I had no idea what I was doing.

Savannah pursed her lips together. "How'd it go?"

"Awkward," I said, shrugging, for it was the truth. "You're not missing out on much."

"Good to know," Savannah said, flopping onto her back and gazing at me with curious eyes. "Can I ask one more question?"

I nodded slowly. "Go for it."

"Why me?"

This question caught me off guard. There wasn't an easy answer for it. "I don't know," I admitted. "Perhaps

Alonsia saw something in you, something pure and *right.* Perhaps you could be just what this world needs."

Savannah snorted. "Absolutely no pressure or anything."

I couldn't have agreed more.

~*~

Another week passed by before I finally heard from my father again, and when I did, his voice sent a shiver down my spine.

I came to Ebonrowe, he said. Straight and to the point. No formalities, no greeting, no nothing.

I would be lying if I didn't admit his lack of a greeting hurt just a tiny bit. After all, we hadn't seen each other in days, and would it kill him to ask how his only son was doing? But no, everything was always business with him.

Nice to hear from you too, Dad.

I didn't realize I had sent that thought to him until I felt my father's consciousness stir, the telltale sign of an alpha trying to keep himself together. *Do you want to hear what I have to say or not?*

I sighed. *Go ahead.*

There is no foreign wolf on or near our lands. I haven't sensed one, and neither have the other wolves. My father paused, and just when I was about to tell him off, that he had to be wrong, he continued. *Callum, it's not a foreign wolf that plagues that village. It's a curse.*

My heart sank upon hearing those words, because he had to be wrong. He just *had* to be. The closest witch coven there were the Witches of Old, and they lived a good two-week's journey from here.

I shook my head. *You're wrong.* He had to be.

My father sighed. *I went to the village. I sniffed the curse myself. My senses don't lie. Werewolves plague the village of Ebonrowe, and there is nothing any of us can do to stop them.*

Werewolf. There was that damn word again, a being all shifters despised. None of them hated werewolves as much as the wolf shifters, however, the one creation that people got mixed up with *us*. Even *Savannah* had called me a werewolf before.

You need to come home, my father said. *There's nothing more you can do.*

That was where he was wrong, however. There were still loads I could do, if only so I could keep Savannah safe. Despite a part of me still refusing to believe werewolves had anything to do with this, the rest of me thought it made sense. The attacks only happened during a full moon. Werewolves could only *shift* during a full moon.

The wounds had clearly been wolf-caused, and it would also explain how Savannah had been unable to catch the creature all this time.

A werewolf—possibly multiple werewolves—plagued her village. And now, I was left trying to figure out how to break this news to Savannah.

FIFTEEN

SAVANNAH

"We need to talk."

Immediately, ice formed in my veins at those four simple words. They were the same words my father said right after we came home from seeing my brother's corpse. It was before they asked me countless questions, trying to piece together what had happened the night before.

"Did you know he left?"

"Where did he go?"

"How could this have happened?"

All the questions blurred together, and I had never

wanted to scream more than I did in that moment. At first, I lied, saying I didn't know anything, but of course, they saw through the lie.

So, I told the truth, that he wanted to have fun with his friends the night before his birthday. The question that was asked afterwards was the one that shattered me into a million tiny pieces.

"Why didn't you stop him?"

And I was frozen in place because I didn't have an answer for that. And then, all I remembered was sobbing recklessly, blubbering because I couldn't string a few words together to save my life.

That question still haunted me to this day, even if my parents didn't blame me for his death. *"Why didn't you stop him?"*

In my experience, the words "we need to talk" never led to anything good. But instead of my parents, this time it was Callum stringing the words together.

And he was staring right at me, his expression made of stone. I hated not knowing what to expect, especially when it came from someone I cared about.

Callum, to his credit, didn't look mad—and I hated to admit how much relief that sent down my spine. But he did look a little sad, and I got the distinct feeling what came next would be hard for him to say.

He's rejecting you, a cruel voice whispered in my subconscious. But that wouldn't make sense, not with how broken he had looked when I had joked with him. Besides, a part of me knew rejecting the bond would hurt him way more than it would hurt me, considering I barely even understood it myself.

Something told me it would destroy him, and I doubted he would do that to himself.

"My dad contacted me today," Callum said, and suddenly, everything began to make sense.

This was about my village, about the damn foreign wolf who dared to threaten it.

This should've been good news. Callum should've been ecstatic to tell me about the bastard who kept slaughtering my people. *So, why did he look downright depressed?*

The only other thing I could think of was the wolf turned out not to be a foreign wolf at all but was instead a member of his pack. My lips pulled into a frown with every silent second that ticked between us because then, that would make Callum the enemy again, and I didn't think I could go back to that.

But there was no other explanation, and if it turned out it *was* one of the wolves from his pack, would he be able to hand them over so I could kill them?

"He wasn't able to sense a foreign wolf, and neither did anyone else in our pack," Callum continued, looking as if each word pained him. "So, he came here. To Ebonrowe."

I blinked, sure I had misheard him. After all, there was no way his father, the esteemed alpha of his pack, would dare come here without a good reason.

Unless he was the one who had been slaughtering our people, a traitorous voice whispered deep inside my subconscious. But that couldn't be true. Fate wouldn't be that cruel.

But then, Callum dropped the bombshell, causing a raging storm to brew in my gut. "It's not a wolf or any animal that plagues your village," he said slowly as if I were something feral and wild, "but a curse."

And just like that, my body wasn't my own as a loud scream ripped out of me before I lunged at Callum, nails extended. Because at this point, he *had* to be protecting his pack. It was the only reason he'd lie to me.

Callum even *said* there wasn't a witch coven for miles, and witches tended to stay out of human affairs. It didn't make any sense.

"Savannah!" Callum yelled, reaching out to block his face as my nails descended upon him. "Savannah, stop!"

A wicked chuckle burst out of my mouth, the sound so unlike anything I've ever produced that I for the moment was taken aback. "Is that your game?" I snarled. "Get me to lower my guard with some fruitless lie so your pack can pick us off one-by-one?"

Callum caught my wrists in his hand with inhuman reflexes. Because of *course* his reflexes would surpass mine. "I'm not lying!" he protested. "Why would I lie to you?"

"I don't know," I said. "To protect your pack and let them continue—"

"I'm telling the truth!"

But Callum had to have known I was lost at that point, twisting my wrists so the slightest bit of pain engulfed them. So I couldn't move. "What the hell do you even know?" I huffed, angry tears blurring my vision. "You're just a goddamn werewolf!"

And just like that, the temperature dropped as if someone suddenly flicked a switch. "No, I'm a wolf *shifter*," Callum said coldly, sending shivers down my spine. "We are born, just like you, and we have control over our shifting abilities. But werewolves *have* no control, for they are the product of a curse. A very dark and evil curse." He paused, his eyes softening. "Made specifically to punish humans."

And just like that, my entire world started spinning as black dots swarmed in my vision. The familiar sense of panic seized control of my heart, filling my veins with its poison, as I fought for each burning breath I took. I opened my mouth, but no sound came out, as I collapsed against Callum's strong chest.

And then, the darkness finally claimed me, and I remembered nothing.

SIXTEEN

CALLUM

The first time I had heard about werewolves was when I was thirteen years old. It had been a part of my homeschooling, a carefully-curated curriculum all wolf shifters in my pack had to go through before adulthood. My tutor had been someone by the name of Sasha Childress, and at the time, she was someone I looked up to constantly.

At that point, I had already known about our history, about how the humans had betrayed us and were swiftly punished for it. And I had known vaguely that witches had doled out their own separate punishments with approval from the goddesses, but it wasn't until then when I learned among those punishments was the werewolf curse, the worst of the worst.

It was a curse meant only for the worst of the settlements, a means of constantly reminding them of how they had wronged us. Yet without their memory, the curse served as the opposite effect, and thus, the beings humans came to know as werewolves oftentimes got confused with *us*. Because not once did humans think werewolves were actually their own cursed peers, travelling through the bloodline so the curse never died out.

I remembered how much hearing about the werewolf curse haunted me. After all, the humans of today had nothing to do with the sins of their ancestors. But witches were vengeful creatures when they wanted to be, so it made sense why they would curse entire bloodlines.

And apparently, Ebonrowe had at one point been one of those settlements, one that relished in torturing our kind. It frightened me to think Savannah's own town had at one point thought nothing of us but vessels for their own cruel experiments.

I shouldn't have been surprised when Savannah fainted right in front of me, her body overcome by panic once again. But for some reason, I was, the image of her collapsing playing over and over again in my mind. A part of me wanted to laugh at the cruel trick Alonsia must've been playing on me, to send me a fated *human* mate that had spawned from one of the worst human settlements during the time of our darkness. But the other part of me, a much stronger part, reminded me that Savannah was *good* and that it was possible for a good seed to be born from evil.

Even when she had almost killed me, she was acting of her own self-preservation and grief, to make sure the fate that befell her brother never happened to anyone else. And then, instead of letting me bleed out, she brought me here to heal, and even when she suspected *I* was the beast who had killed her brother, she never finished the job she set out to do. Instead, she heard me out and gave me a chance.

I brought Savannah to her bedroom, tucking her body beneath the covers in an attempt to make her as comfortable as possible. I had lived in the supernatural world all my life, but she had just been introduced to it, and if roles had been reversed, I knew I would've had a hard time dealing with everything too. But I couldn't offer her any more than blatant comfort until she finally woke from her slumber.

And then, I would have a lot of explaining to do. And I would have to figure out a way to make this curse easier for her to digest. Because unlike me, she hasn't had years to process this part of the world. Until I came along, she lived in blissful ignorance of everything.

It seemed like hours before she finally came to, and when she did, she gave a soft moan as if she were in pain. Her body twitched as she stirred, breathing deeply, as if she were in the most peaceful slumber.

My fingers itched to touch her, to move strands of her hair from her face, my hand reaching out before I could think otherwise. I glided my fingers lightly over her skin, imagining her leaning into my touch.

No, not imagined—she *was* leaning into my touch as if she had been starved without it. Her eyelids fluttered, a content sigh escaping her lips, before slowly blinking at me.

A lazy smile stretched across her lips as our gazes met, and for the first time, she looked…happy. As if she hadn't been plagued by monsters all her life.

I didn't think anything could be as perfect as that one single moment, and a pang formed in my chest, squeezing my heart. It was something I hadn't experienced with anyone else, something that hurt almost as much as it gave pleasure.

Mate, my wolf chimed, itching to claim her as ours. And for a moment, I allowed him to guide us forward to finally cement the bond.

No! another part of me cried, a very *human* part. *Not yet!* My wolf whined as I denied him what should've been his by default, but he needed to understand humans were different from wolves.

Consent was a human concept, after all, something my wolf didn't fully understand. But I did, and as such, I would not allow him to claim her while she was still recovering from a panic attack.

"Callum?" she called breathlessly, almost sleepily, skirting her hand up until it pinned mine against her cheek.

"Hmm?" I hummed as my wolf retreated back into itself.

Savannah's smile grew. "Kiss me."

My wolf howled against my rib cage, sure that was what humans meant when they came up with *consent*, but I knew better. Her body was still recovering, her mind still in a delirious state, so I shook my head. "Not yet."

Savannah pulled her lips into a frown. "Why not?"

I chuckled at her persistence. "Believe me, my wolf would like nothing more than to claim you as his," I said, "but you're just coming out of another panic attack. It wouldn't be right."

Savannah scrunched her face. "Huh," she said. "So, *that's* what this is."

"Yes." I took my hand away, and she practically whined at the lost contact. "You need to rest, let your body catch up to the rest of you."

Savannah smirked. "You *do* care!"

"Never said I didn't," I said, bemused. "My wolf, on the other hand—"

"Shut up!" she chastised. "You're lying!"

I belted out a laugh before shuffling towards the door. "I'm going to get you some water." Because it was important to stay hydrated, especially after a panic attack.

At least, I *thought* it was important. I admittedly didn't have much experience when it came to panic attacks.

By the time I returned with a glass of water in hand, Savannah was sitting up in bed with an open book propped on her lap. She barely glanced up as I set the glass on her nightstand, her finger gliding along the pages as she read.

"Whatcha reading?" I questioned, taking a seat beside

her.

Savannah shifted the book so the cover was facing me. "Trevor got it for me."

I didn't know who Trevor was, but a different kind of pang formed in my gut this time. A pang born of jealousy. My wolf rattled against its skeletal cage, demanding to be let out, to find this Trevor and show him exactly who Savannah belonged to.

No! I scolded him, my human side able to think more rationally. Perhaps this Trevor character was just a friend or a cousin or—

Who am I kidding? I wailed, fists clenching. We weren't technically a thing, so she could see whomever she wished, but I would be lying if I didn't admit picturing her wrapped around another guy sent my head spinning.

Somehow, despite this war raging inside me, I was able to remain calm. "*The Chesterfield Curse?*" I questioned, looking for anything to distract me. "Is it good?"

"It's good," Savannah said nonchalantly. Then, she stuck a piece of paper into the book and closed it. "You can admit it, you know."

"Admit what?" I said, playing dumb.

Savannah traded the book for her glass of water, bringing it to her lips and taking a huge sip. "That you're jealous," she said. "It's practically radiating off you in waves. You're not doing as good a job hiding it as you think you are."

I shook my head. "I don't know what you're talking

about." *Real smooth, Callum!*

"Suit yourself." Savannah paused, taking another sip. "Trevor's not my boyfriend, by the way. He is—*was*—a very close friend."

My shoulders sagged in relief as if of their own accord. "Was?" I inquired. "Not anymore?"

"I don't know," Savannah said. "He wants more than I can give him, and I don't think we can ever go back to being friends." There was a touch of sadness in her voice, chasing away the rest of my jealousy.

"I'm sorry," I said. Because I didn't know what else to say. "Were you two ever..."

"We gave it a shot, like, last year sometime, but it didn't work out." Savannah shrugged like it was no big deal. "And nothing has been the same between us ever since."

But I was able to read between the lines. It *was* a big deal to her, even if she couldn't admit it. Losing a friend was always hard, no matter the circumstances.

If I somehow lost Sammy, I didn't know what I would do.

So, I just sat there and offered her comfort as she drank her water. For a moment, it was as if nothing had happened, as if she had always been like this, not suffering from a massive panic attack.

Until she turned to face me, her lips pursed. "What's this curse you were telling me about?"

Shit! I swore. The last thing I wanted was to spiral down the same path that led to her panic attack in the first place. "I don't think talking about this is a good idea," I stated bluntly. "Need I remind you—"

"This concerns my village, Callum," Savannah snapped. "I deserve to know!"

"You just had another massive panic attack!" I argued, causing her to blanch. I lowered my voice. "You're not ready."

Savannah scoffed. "First off, *I* decide if I'm ready, and second—"

"Savannah!" I whined, staring at her in disbelief. This was a woman who would have a total meltdown one minute and then be fine the next, never having the same trigger twice. Perhaps her panic was just what she needed to prepare herself to hear the rest, in a sense getting it out of her system.

But I still wasn't so convinced she *could* handle what I had to tell her, despite what she otherwise claimed.

"You were claiming my village is cursed," Savannah went on, ignoring my plea. "I need to know exactly what I'm up against."

A sigh tumbled out of my lips. I knew she was right, and if it were that simple, I'd tell her in a heartbeat, but… "How do I know you won't have another panic attack?"

"You don't." Savannah shrugged. "But that's a risk I'm willing to take."

"Yeah, well, that's not a risk *I'm* willing to take," I spat.

"Callum!"

"Savannah," I shot back at her. "Be reasonable. Please."

"I *am* being reasonable!"

"No, you're not!" I argued, my face softening. "What happened was one of the scariest things of my life. To see you suffering, a victim of your own limited mind—"

"My mind is *not* limited!"

"It is when it comes to this," I said. "Savannah, please!"

Unfortunately for me, my mate was one of the most stubborn females I had ever met, second only to my own mother. "Nah, I think I'd rather take my chances," she said. "After all, humans already know about werewolves."

"Not like this." I shook my head. "Your people often confuse them with *us.*"

"Considering how defensive you get whenever I call you a werewolf, yeah, I figured." Savannah paused. "Now, what was it you were saying before I blacked out? Werewolves are actually a curse meant to punish us?"

Shit, I guess we're doing this now. I sucked in a deep breath. "Before I say anything else, you have to understand how traumatizing the dark years were, when humans practically enslaved us. Witches were caught in the crossfire trying to help us and maintain the peace, but by the end, peace was something we could no longer achieve while humans still knew about us."

Savannah shivered. I could tell this part of our history bothered her, further cementing the thought that she was too *good* for this otherwise fucked-up world. "I know," she said. "I mean, I don't *really* know, not like you, but…" Her words trailed off.

169

I took her hand in mine, the one that wasn't holding a glass of water. "Some human settlements were worse than others. We're talking straight-up torture."

Savannah froze. "What are you trying to say?"

There was no easy way to say this, which was why I wanted to wait to tell her. But she gave me no choice, and I found I couldn't deny her even if I wanted to. "Ebonrowe at one point had been like that, one of the worst of the worst," I began slowly, hoping my quiet speech would soften the blow. "Humans weren't just punished by our goddesses. In some cases, the witches doled out their own punishments."

"What are you trying to say?" Savannah repeated, though now, there was a touch of fear to her voice. I wanted to stop, wanted to assure her I would tell her in time but that she wasn't ready yet, but I knew she wouldn't let me get away that easily.

So, I sucked it up and said in a rush, "In settlements like yours, the witches thought it necessary to punish them further, to remind those humans of their sins. They created the werewolf curse specifically *for* that, a spell that passes from generation to generation through a familial line. Someone or multiple people in your village have been afflicted by this, causing them to transform into a wolf-like creature every full moon."

Savannah stilled as realization dawned on her face. "Werewolves," she stated breathlessly. "The ones we came to know?"

"The wolf-like humanoids? Exactly." I nodded.

Savannah shook her head. "So, you're telling me one of the citizens here, someone I probably knew my entire life, is the reason for our village's suffering?"

Again, I nodded. "But they wouldn't know. Those who are cursed don't remember their time as the beast. To them, they wake up each morning as if nothing is amiss," I explained. "Which makes them extremely dangerous."

Savannah blinked. "How do I stop it?"

"Kill the afflicted," I said as if the answer should've been obvious. "Destroy their entire family line. But in order to do that, you have to actually know who's afflicted first, which is extremely difficult."

"But not impossible," Savannah mused. "You'll help me, right?"

I stared at her, dumbfounded. "Savannah, you can't be serious! This curse is dangerous!"

Savannah's expression hardened. "If the only way to free my village is to throw myself into the line of fire, then I have to do it! With or without you!"

"Fuck, why can't you just listen to me for once?" I shouted before realizing what I just said. My eyes widened in horror. My wolf had gotten way too close to the surface, his protectiveness feeding into my own. "Shit, Savannah, I'm so sorry. My wolf—"

"Save it!" she snipped, yanking her hand from mine and holding it up. "I have to do this, Callum. Now that I know what *it* is, I have to try!"

"I know," I said solemnly. "Damn it, I know!" I wanted

to throw things, break whatever I could find, tear the whole world down around us until there was nothing left. But I couldn't do any of that. I couldn't lose myself to the wolf in front of her because then, she would never want to be around me again. The fact she still hasn't run for the hills was a downright miracle.

It was clear I wouldn't be able to talk her out of this suicide mission, and the only other way to keep her safe would be to help her. And that last option wouldn't guarantee her safety.

For the first time ever, I cursed the witches who had done this, spearing her with a determined gaze. "Fine, I'll help you." I paused, letting my words sink in. "But you let *me* do most of the frontline work. This is non-negotiable."

Savannah nodded. "I understand." Then, she flashed me a cheeky smile. "But by the end of this, you may find it is *you* who will have trouble keeping up with *me*."

SEVENTEEN

SAVANNAH

Despite my bravado, I hadn't the faintest idea of where to start. Even though Ebonrowe was small, there were still a good couple hundred people living here, and to sift through them all, trying to pinpoint a curse I wasn't even sure how to sniff out would be damn near impossible.

So much for me thinking this would be a piece of cake...

As much as I hated to admit it, I may actually need Callum in sniffing out the curse. He was the ever-vigilant wolf at my side, sniffing around for the faintest whiff of something amiss. And due to his huge stature, plenty of people gave us a wide berth, but that didn't stop him from taking a whiff in their general directions, shaking his head when he came up empty.

Nothing, he said after what felt like the millionth time, growing impatient. I couldn't blame him, because I was growing impatient too. I wanted to end my village's curse as quickly as possible.

I'm going as quickly as I can! Callum's voice practically slammed into my mind, and I winced. But more than that, I was struck with the painful realization that he could *get inside my head!*

"What the fuck?" I swore under my breath, not at all amused.

I could practically hear Callum's chuckle as he said, *It's a mate thing.*

"You mean to tell me you could get into my head this entire time?" I hissed. "My thoughts are private!"

Not when you practically broadcast them to me, Callum said matter-of-factly. *I especially like the ones that are about me and how devilishly handsome—*

Callum! I screeched, though only a second passed before I realized I had used the weird mind-speak thingy as well. And to my amazement, it felt just as natural as talking out loud.

Callum snickered. *I could always teach you how to block me so not every thought is broadcasted, but what would be the fun in that?*

Shut up! I screamed, pressing my hands to my ears as if

that would stop the flow of Callum's taunts.

You do realize that won't work, right? Callum questioned, sounding almost bored. *Hello, mind-speak, because our minds are linked. You can't escape me that easily.*

Let's just focus on the task at hand, I grumbled, lowering my hands. I must look crazy, with my hands shielding my ears from a sound no one else could hear.

You could say that again. Callum scoffed.

I rolled my eyes and then proceeded to ignore him as we continued meandering through town. Thankfully, my parents were at work today, so they wouldn't be able to question why I suddenly had an over-one-hundred-pound wolf practically glued to my hip. I *could* pass him off as a pet, but would my parents let me keep him?

Maybe if I begged really, *really* hard, my parents wouldn't mind. He could help fill the void my brother left behind.

Except nothing about Callum screamed *brother* to me.

You're not a sister to me either, Callum sang, causing my cheeks to redden. *Especially after—*

"Okay!" I shouted out loud, everyone in our proximity suddenly turning towards me as if I had just sprouted two heads. The blush deepened as embarrassment took hold. "What!" I snapped. "Ever seen a wolf before?"

That caused everyone to whirl around quickly, all except for one, who continued staring at me as if I wasn't real.

Fucking hell!

Trevor Browning closed the gap between us, eyeing Callum as if he would at any moment jump up and attack him. "Hey, Sav," he greeted warily. "Nice, uh…wolf."

"Thanks," I grumbled, shifting awkwardly from one foot to the next.

"Is this where your prize money went?" Trevor shook his head. "Honestly, Sav, if you wanted a pet this badly, you could've just gotten a dog from the—"

"Wolves are so much better," I said nervously, cutting him off. "This one always keeps me on my toes. I never know if he's feeling nice or grumpy most days."

I'm always nice, Callum supplied.

You have your moments, wolf! I shot back.

"So, uh, what's its name?" Trevor rubbed the back of his neck, still staring at Callum nervously.

"Rex," I said with no hesitation. "Isn't that right, Rex?"

Seriously? You couldn't have picked a more awesome and non-basic name? Callum complained. *Everybody and their mothers name their pets Rex. Whatever happened to Hercules or Dimitri or even—*

You better shut it or else I'll change your name to Sapphire, I warned, plastering on a fake smile as I patted him on the head. "Such a good boy, Rex! You actually managed *not* to eat the first human we came across for once!"

Trevor paled. "Only you would buy a cannibalistic wolf."

"Technically, it isn't cannibalism if it's a wolf and it eats people," I supplied. "Now, if it ate other wolves, then yes, but not—"

"Okay, I get it." Trevor held up both hands. "Just make sure your *carnivorous* pet doesn't think I'll be his next meal!"

I don't know. He's looking mighty tasty right about now. As if for emphasis, Callum sniffed the air around Trevor before blanching, as if he just smelled something fowl. *Never mind.*

"Well, nice seeing you, Savannah!" Trevor waved, bolting out of there so fast I could've sworn I saw the outline of a person where he once stood.

As fun as that was, Callum began once Trevor was out of sight, *we have a slight problem.*

I groaned. *What now?*

I'm assuming that was Trevor? Callum guessed.

Yes. Why? I inquired.

He smells funny.

My eyes widened. *No. No way! I've been friends with Trevor for a really long time! I would know if he were cursed!*

My nose doesn't lie, Callum said. *Besides, I thought you two* weren't *friends anymore.*

It's…complicated. I sighed. *I'd like to be, but there's too much baggage between us. I don't think we could ever go back to being casual friends.*

Believe me, I could smell his arousal too, Callum said. *That boy is definitely* not *over you.*

First off, ew. Please don't ever tell me again if a boy is aroused because of me, I scolded. *Second of all, I* know *jealousy can hinder your senses. You're wrong this time, Callum!*

My nose never lies, Callum sang one more time as if

taunting me. *But I'd have to catch a whiff of the rest of his family just to make sure.*

I shook my head but said nothing. Because even though I doubted wholeheartedly that Trevor's family was cursed, it was a lead. *Finally, a lead!*

That's the spirit!

I glared at Callum. *You know, I'm starting to regret letting you loose.*

You wound me, Sav! Callum scoffed.

Immediately, I froze. *What did you just call me?* Only one person had ever called me that, and it was Trevor. No one else had even been *allowed* to do so, and yet—

Sav, Callum said. *Trevor called you that, and I kinda liked it, so...*

So unoriginal, I groaned. *To steal someone else's nickname for me.*

Fine. What about Banana? Callum supplied.

Banana? I scrunched my face.

Yeah. As in Savanna Banana! Callum practically howled in laughter.

Oh my god! I screeched, sure my face was turning red once again. *You know, on second thought...Sav is just fine.*

Too late...Banana, Callum said, much to my chagrin.

My hands balled into tight fists, but even I couldn't help the smile that swept across my lips. *Shut it, Rex, or I might just kick you!*

Callum gasped. *You wouldn't!*

I laughed maniacally. *I totally would!* I paused. *By the*

way, you're sleeping outside tonight.

Now, that's just cruel! Callum whined. *You would dare deprive me of a nice, warm bed?*

I shook my head. *Spoiled wolf!*

Even more spoiled Banana, Callum grumbled.

Before he could utter another word, I kicked him. Not hard, but enough to know I meant business, because who would I be if I didn't keep my word? Callum doubled over in fake pain as I pounced on him, drawing him to my chest.

You wound me, Banana! Callum repeated, this time using my new "original" nickname. *And here, I thought we were past all the physical abuse!*

I belted out a laugh. *Please, I barely even scratched you!*

Mark my words, Banana, Callum warned lightheartedly. *Soon, I will have my revenge.*

~*~

Callum ended up *not* sleeping outside that night. It turned out I had more of a heart than I realized. Either that, or I just *really* craved his heat. But like the spoiled wolf he was, he spent the night snuggled up beside me in human form.

In my bed.

Underneath *my* covers.

Damn spoiled werewolf!

Beside me, Callum groaned, and for an instant, I forgot he could tap into my mind. *For the last time, I am not a werewolf!* he chastised.

A grin split my lips. *You'll always be* my *werewolf.* And then, I wanted to flinch at how cheesy that sounded. *Oh, god, what did you do to me?*

I did nothing to you...Banana, Callum said.

Can you please *stop calling me that?* I whined.

No. Straight and to the point.

Why not?

Because it's fun. In an instant, Callum burst into high-pitched laughter, causing my ears to ring.

You know, the offer to sleep outside still stands, I teased, shooting him my best glare.

Callum shuddered. *No thank you.*

I shifted my body so I was facing him. "Is that fear I sense?" I laughed. "Who would've known the big, bad wolf shifter was afraid of the outdoors?"

Callum raised an eyebrow. "We're speaking out loud now?" he questioned, amused. "And here I thought we were having fun mind-speaking to each other!"

I scoffed. "For you, maybe, but for me, it's still weird. And I still need to learn how to block you out!"

"Oh, Savannah," Callum tsked. "Whatever am I going to do with you?"

"You'd be out in the cold, for one thing," I said, scrutinizing his built form. All Callum was wearing was a set of plaid boxer shorts I managed to swipe from my dad, his lean chest on full display. My eyes dipped lower to the trail of blonde hairs that disappeared into the waistband of the boxers. Heat clenched my core, traveling up through my body.

Heat I was so *not* used to. *Fuck do I need a cold shower...and some much-needed space.*

A mischievous smirk split Callum's lips. "Say that again?"

"For fuck's sake!" I scowled, rolling over so my back was to him. "Stay out of my head!"

"Like I said, it's hard when you practically broadcast your thoughts to me."

I rolled my eyes even though he couldn't see it. "It's not too late to kick you out, you know."

Callum fake-shuddered. "Please don't. I promise to be good from now on!"

I shook my head. "Why don't you put on a shirt?"

"You didn't give me one," he deadpanned.

Oh, right. I sighed. *Minor detail.*

"Not that I really mind, per se," Callum continued, and soon, I felt the lightest of touches skim my clothed back, sending shivers down my spine. "My only lament is that you're wearing more than me."

"Oh no!" I said. "You are not *manipulating* me into—"

"Who said anything about manipulating you?" For his part, Callum sounded wounded, his fingers stilling on my back. "You can do whatever you want. I'm just observing things."

"No, you're trying to subtly tell me to shed my nightgown!" I ground out, cocking my head over my shoulder and meeting his amused stare. "Newsflash: it's not happening!"

Callum resumed tracing shapes along my back. "You will find, Savannah, that nudity is a commonality amongst shifters. After all, why wear clothing if we're just going to shred through it when we shift?"

"You'll find humans don't *quite* have the same sentiment," I grumbled.

Callum sighed. "Such a shame, to cover up that which you were gifted. I'll never understand human conservatism."

I scoffed. "Well, us humans will never understand you shifters and your nudity, so…ditto!"

Callum gave a hearty laugh before quieting, developing a far-away look. As if he were thinking. Worry creased his brow, and it was so unlike him, so unlike the sense of joking familiarity we've established, that my head started spinning.

"What's wrong?" I asked sincerely, shifting so I faced him again.

Callum's gaze flicked to me, offering a small smile purely for my benefit. "Nothing," he said. "Just thinking."

But I knew there was more to it. I didn't know how I knew, but I just *knew* in that weird psychic kinda way people got sometimes.

Something must've shown on my face because Callum quickly added, "I'm just worried about my pack. Nothing major."

But it was major for him. I could see the truth in his

eyes. Until now, I didn't realize how much weeks away from his pack would feel to him, especially when he was in line to become the next alpha. He probably had duties he needed to attend to that he was neglecting because he was helping me.

"Your father knows you're here. He's even *been* here," I pointed out. "Why hasn't he tried to take you back yet?"

Callum's eyes glazed over in thought. "Because he's not like one of those ruthless alphas who thinks everyone should worship the ground they walk on. Because despite the rigorous training he puts me through, he respects my decisions." He paused, his voice growing quiet. "And because he knows I've found my mate."

My stomach churned at the last bit, though in an excited-nervous kind of way. It was strange to think something that would've sent my heart spiraling into a panic mere days ago was now something I relished.

"I think I've mentioned how huge the fated mate bond is to us, how much Alonsia's decisions mean to us," Callum continued. "My father wouldn't dare come between that no matter *who* I was mated to: wolf, a different shifter species, human, or even a witch."

"Good to know," I said. The last thing I needed was a protective father thwarting me at every turn. Who also happened to be the alpha of the closest wolf pack to my village. I didn't need to add that to my growing list of things to watch out for.

"In any case," Callum said on a sigh, "I can still worry."

I didn't know what to say or even if I *could* say anything to make the situation better, so I just curled further into him, listening to his steady, rapid heartbeat. And it tore me up inside that I could feel *everything*, every tiny morsel of pain and self-loathing he inflicted onto himself.

I didn't remember when I fell asleep, but when I woke up the next morning, my bed felt strangely empty, my body devoid of warmth. Callum was gone, as if he had been a dream all along.

And I was alone.

EIGHTEEN

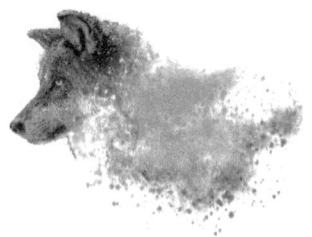

CALLUM

It had been days since I last enjoyed a run as my wolf, not since the interrupted one I had with Sammy before Savannah found me. I couldn't believe I had forgotten how freeing it was, to feel the air whip through my fur as I sprinted deep into the forest, the subtlest, woodsy scents surrounding me in what could only be described as *home*.

Shifters in general had always been the fondest of nature, our dwellings carved within the Earth itself, depending on the shifter species. As wolves, my pack used wood, manipulating it into the beautiful structures that dotted our landscape. Since the forest was our home, we didn't have access to much else, though I've heard stories of other wolf shifter packs having carved their homes into great mountains.

Ever since I was a kid, I had longed to see one, had longed to climb some of the highest peaks while visiting other shifter territories for diplomacy. My dad used to go on long diplomacy trips when I was younger before I began my official training, always entertaining me with great stories of mountain lion shifters and eagle shifters and the places they chose to make their home. He promised me I would someday embark on those journeys and see all the world had to offer.

Now that I was older, thoughts of traveling were just wishful thinking. As alpha, I wouldn't be allowed a day off to explore, not when I had an entire pack of wolves depending on me twenty-four-seven,

Which was what made this expedition to Ebonrowe extra weird. I normally wasn't one to shirk my duties as the future alpha, but this town's curse seemed important somehow. Almost like it engraved itself into me, sewing itself into my very soul until I helped Savannah solve its mystery.

And that was *before* Ebonrowe defied the expected in the form of a fated mate. A *human* fated mate.

No wonder I needed a run...

I had been so caught up in everything, I barely paid any attention to my wolf's needs. The poor fellow has been cooped up inside, begging for release, but I thought nothing of it, consumed with what my life had now become. In fact, it wasn't until I woke up this morning before the sun rose with Savannah slung over my torso that I finally felt the unbearable itching, as if a swarm of fleas had taken refuge in my gut. This had quickly been followed by my wolf's ghostly howl, rattling my bones to the core.

So, I untangled myself from Savannah as gently as I could so as not to wake her, stripped out of the boxer shorts she gave me, shifted, and took off into the surrounding woods. And now, here I was two hours later, still running, still trying to expel my wolf's boundless energy.

I would *never* keep him cooped up again, that was for damn sure.

A few more minutes into my run, a gnarly, unfamiliar smell accosted me, causing me to come to a full stop. It wasn't the signature scent of prey or another wolf or even the forest in general, but something else. Something...gross.

Magic! I quickly realized. It was indeed the smell of magic, like sulfur mixed with rotten eggs, the signature scent of a witch. My hackles instantly rose, because a witch would have no reason to come all the way out here, unless...

No, I scolded myself. There was no way a witch came for a curse that was almost as old as time itself. Witches didn't involve themselves with humans anymore. At least, that was what I had been taught. But I couldn't escape the reality of what I was smelling, and it couldn't be anything good.

Warily, I followed the scent, now at a relaxing trot as I scanned the forest for anything that seemed amiss. And within seconds, I came across the offender, a spindly woman with pale, leathery skin that stretched over protruding bones, long, stringy, black hair falling into the witch's face. She wore a hunch in her back, claws protruding from her hands instead of nails, and her bare, crow-like feet were filthy, seeming to dig into the earth as if she could topple over at any minute. This was a woman who let magic consume her very soul, warping her in a way that made her look monstrous, her thin, frail body barely supporting the torn, black dress she had on.

There had once been a witch in my pack who acted as a healer for a few years during the time I was a toddler. I barely remembered her, but what I *did* remember was that she didn't look anywhere near this willowy. Later in my studies, I had learned witches could glamor themselves to look more human-like, but they only really did so if they knew they were traveling to places that weren't used to their kind.

But this witch didn't even try to hide what she was, as if she didn't count on being seen by anyone. And that was the scary part. Witches had no beef with shifters, but they weren't ones to let go of grudges easily. I had no doubt this witch came from the closest coven to Ebonrowe, the Witches of Old, sent to investigate the town.

And the only reason they would bother doing so was if they knew something wasn't right, that someone was snooping around, trying to undo their hard work. In this case, that someone would be Savannah and I. *We* had caused this witch to be here, and my breath hitched as I realized Savannah and I weren't nearly careful enough.

I'd be damned if this witch harmed even a single hair on Savannah's head.

Clearing my throat, I shifted back into my human form, bones popping as they twisted and contorted. The witch's back was still facing me, but somehow, I knew she knew she was no longer alone.

The witch sniffed the air, slowly turning around, glowing orbs of yellow shining through her matted hair as her eyes locked onto me. "Begone, wolf!" she commanded. "This doesn't concern you!"

I stayed where I was, meeting her stare as if we were locked in a competitive staring contest. And the witch, I hated to admit, was winning.

When I remained silent, the witch took a step forward, one clawed foot snapping a branch in half. "Are you deaf?" she demanded. "I said begone!"

I knew I had to say something. Otherwise, this witch would probably think there was something wrong with my voice. Eventually, I managed to find my voice enough to belt out, "Why are you here, witch?"

The witch halted her movements and cocked her head to the side. "Interesting," she commented, seeming for a moment lost in her own little world. "I didn't expect to run into Xander Woodsworth's son out here, so far from home."

This threw me for a loop, because how in the fuck did this random witch know who I was? I schooled my features into what I hoped was an expression of nonchalance, but I couldn't tell with the panic threatening to take over my body.

The witch barked out a sharp laugh. "Don't be so surprised!" she said. "Your father and I go way back, since before you were even born. I used to visit quite frequently, you know, before my bones became even frailer."

"My father never told me this," I admitted, feeling ashamed. He had never been one to share details about his life before me, but somehow, the fact he never told me cut deep like a knife.

The witch waved me off. "He wouldn't, dearie," she huffed. "My, I haven't been back here in well over fifty years."

I stiffened. "Then, why are you here?"

The witch ignored me. "You look just like him, you know, when he was younger." She paused, a grin splitting her lips. "I'm Sahara, by the way."

Sahara. No last name, since witches didn't have one. Their coven was their family, so it was always something like Sahara of the Witches of Old. For the first time that morning, goosebumps peppered my skin, though it wasn't due to the chilly wind. I could practically feel the power radiating off Sahara, probing, testing. Trying to infiltrate my senses until I lived and breathed the magic, allowing her access to every single thought, every single desire. Witches were dangerous creatures, and I was glad they for the most part were on the same side as shifters with a few rogue covens here and there.

"To answer your question, child, my coven sends a representative here every year to make sure our handiwork is still intact," Sahara finally explained. "Usually, it's our coven leader, Willow, but she has fallen ill, so I was sent in her steed." She paused, her eyes raking over me as if she couldn't quite figure something out. "I fear her time is coming to an end."

I shuddered at this revelation. Though they weren't immortal, witches had very long lifespans, way longer than humans and shifters. Their lives could span hundreds of years, through multiple generations, their magic growing in power as they aged. If this Willow was nearing her expiration date, I shuddered to think how old and powerful she was.

Witches were *always* female. Hectora made it that way specifically, so magic passed from woman to woman through the maternal line. They had men, yes. Otherwise, they wouldn't be able to reproduce, but the men, called *scarvoks* in the old witch's tongue, were not quite human but weren't gifted magic either.

In human and shifter language, there wasn't a direct translation, but I always thought it could mean "magicless witch." Of course, witchkind would lambast me for that, since in their culture, men had no magic and therefore *couldn't* be considered witches.

It was then when I realized something very important. Unbeknownst to me and Savannah, the Witches of Old have been secretly coming here, making sure their curse was alive and well. The curse Savannah and I were actively trying to break.

An involuntary shudder wracked my spine, but I shifted my bare feet in an attempt to hide it. I couldn't let Sahara in on that fact, because doing so could mean war between her coven and my pack, but not before she skinned Savannah alive.

No one went against the Witches of Old. At least, no one stupid enough, until Savannah and I came along. They were an old and powerful coven, one of the first.

"Willow was the one who initially cast the curse, you know," Sahara continued, seeming unaware of my inner musings. "At the special request of your pack's alpha at the time."

This was news to me, for it signaled my pack and her coven have been close for a while. I always thought witches created the curse for their own form of revenge, but I should've known the Witches of Old would've been different. They were wise, always harping about the natural balance and therefore wouldn't dare mess with it.

Unless they had probable cause, a direct request from a beaten and war-torn pack who carried the scars of what the humans from Ebonrowe did to them.

I should've been ecstatic that my familial line went so far as to strike a deal with the devil in order to guarantee their pack's safety, but all I felt was dread. Dread at the fact the humans of today didn't deserve to pay for their people's past sins. *Savannah* certainly didn't.

Sahara must've sensed something in me, for her smile vanished. "What's troubling you, child?" she inquired in a motherly tone, one I wanted to leap into and never look back.

I shook my head. "Just thinking." Then, as if on cue, a thought *did* come to me. "What's wrong with Willow?"

Sahara's smile returned, though now with a lot less force behind it. "It's a sickness that ails all of us when we're near our deathbed. It's called *qu'untok* in our language, but your kind would probably compare it to an extreme version of the flu. Fever, shakes, the like—it's awful."

"I'm sorry," I said, and I meant it. Shifters rarely got sick, not like humans, but I could only imagine how painful it must be.

"Don't be. Her time has been coming for a while now. We can only hope her handiwork will continue once she finally passes to join our goddess in the afterlife," Sahara said. "Which is why I'm here. What I don't understand, however, is why *you're* here."

"I was out for a run." That, at least, wasn't a lie.

"Yes, I can see that." Sahara practically turned her nose up as her eyes assessed my naked form, disgust rolling through her. Witches were prudish creatures, and like humans, they developed a sense of modesty. Not that it mattered to them, however, since they didn't have to deal with shredded clothing, like we did if we somehow forgot to take something off before shifting.

"But so far from home, Callum?" Sahara pestered. "You've never wandered this far before."

I shrugged. "I figured it would finally be good for me to see the world. Our pack lands are so small, as you know, and I haven't had a chance to really get out there and see everything the world has to offer."

"Is that it?" Sahara pursed her lips together. "Or is it something else?"

I shook my head. "That's it."

"Don't lie to me, child. I can smell the human on you." Sahara crinkled her nose. "What I *can't* discern is *why*, unless...oh, sweet goddess Hectora. You found your mate!"

A blush coated my cheeks, and by that point, I knew it was too late. Any lie I came up with would've fallen on deaf ears, since witches were very good at sniffing out lies.

"Your mate is a human? And not only that, an *Ebonrowe* human?" Sahara questioned, though for her part, she looked more curious than enraged.

This is good, I thought. *It means perhaps she'll be open to hearing me out about the curse.* But when I opened my mouth to speak, the witch plowed on as if I did nothing.

"My, this hasn't happened since before everything went down!" Sahara said cheerily. "Good for you, dearie, even if they're human. Tell me, though, do they know?"

I didn't need her to elaborate to know what she meant, so I simply nodded.

"Well, I'll be! And they haven't tried to chop your head off yet? That's a good start, at least." Sahara sighed wistfully. "For a shifter to find their mate, there's nothing else truly like it, is there?"

It was a rhetorical question, one I knew I didn't need to answer. "Perhaps Alonsia saw something in her," I emphasized. "Saw the *good* in her."

"So, it's a girl, is it?" Sahara smirked cheekily. "Alonsia would've. Otherwise, she never would've paired you two."

"So, you'll do it? Lift the curse, I mean." I didn't know what compelled me to think Sahara thinking nothing of my human mate meant she would lift something that has plagued Ebonrowe for far too long, but when the witch's smirk instantly vanished, I knew it was a lost cause.

"Tell me, child. If you were tortured, damaged beyond repair, wouldn't you want your assailants to suffer a similar fate?" Sahara questioned, raising an eyebrow.

"But you guys weren't the ones who suffered," I protested. "And the humans of today had nothing to do with the sins of their ancestors."

"That may be true, but you weren't alive during the dark years," Sahara said. "Neither was I, for that matter, but Willow was, and all she could do was explain how horrifying it was. It was only a matter of time before humanity discovered and enslaved us too, you know, and I think that fact played a part in Willow's decision to curse Ebonrowe at the alpha's request. That kind of trauma never quite leaves you, and if you were in her position, wouldn't you want the same thing?"

Of course I would. In fact, I *did* at some point, before I met Savannah. Before I knew good humans existed and that they were just as innocent as the rest of us. "There has to be something you can do. Savannah doesn't deserve—" I immediately stopped, my eyes going wide as I just realized what I did. I just disclosed the name of my mate, my very *human* mate, and when it came to witches, names were dangerous.

Sahara must've seen the horror on my face, for she chuckled. "Don't worry. Your mate's safe, so long as the two of you stay out of our business. She won't stay in Ebonrowe forever anyway, since you'll at some point have to infect her with your blood, won't you?"

This was something I hadn't even considered until now, but I should have. As my mate, and if she accepted, she would have to become one of us, a changed wolf. We only did it to *human* mates, for witch blood and the blood of other shifter species would reject our seed, and it wasn't common, since human-wolf pairings hadn't been very common to begin with. Ours was the first I knew of in centuries.

And once I changed her, if she was willing, she would be infertile. Changed wolves were *always* infertile, which meant I would have to delegate someone *else's* child to become the next alpha heir when that time came.

But that still didn't change the fact her people were still suffering for something they had nothing to do with. "Her people are innocent," I tried one last time. "They've suffered long enough."

But Sahara didn't even bat an eyelash. "You'll find, Callum, that no one is truly innocent, not even your mate," she said. "But I'll give you my word. No harm shall befall her or you so long as you both stay out of our affairs."

In other words, we needed to stop trying to break the curse, or else we would have an entire coven of vengeful witches descend upon us in a heartbeat.

"Now, go on! Enjoy the rest of your run." Sahara's easy smile returned. "And do come by the Westfall Mountains at some point. I'm sure Willow would be delighted to see you before she passes."

And then, she vanished in a puff of smoke, leaving behind the dread she planted in my skin with that thinly-veiled threat. One thing became painfully clear. There was no saving Ebonrowe, and if we didn't stop now, we would both be in danger. *Savannah* would be in danger.

And I couldn't let that happen.

~*~

When I finally returned to Ebonrowe, in my wolf form once again, I was met with a very worried and pissed-off Savannah. But I couldn't think straight with the weight of my failure heavily holding me down, wondering how on Earth I was going to break this news to her. I knew she wouldn't take it well, but I would rather her be safe than risk the wrath of the Witches of Old.

So, I let her lead me into her house, feeling very much like a puppy with their tail tucked between their legs. *This was going to be fun…*

Not.

NINETEEN

SAVANNAH

I didn't think I'd ever get used to seeing naked man. The first time was a shock, but now that I knew somewhat of what to expect…

Well, it was still a shock.

My lower half twitched, seeming to be at war with my head, who kept telling me, "No, thank you!" I didn't think I could handle his alien today or…any day, really, but *especially* today.

"I can hear you, you know!" Callum grumbled as he pulled a plain white t-shirt over his head. More clothes I stole from my father. In fact, I was getting quite good at this whole stealing thing.

I scoffed, waving at him with my hands. "Not my fault you keep waving your alien dick around!"

Callum heaved a heavy sigh. "Have you ever *seen* the inside of a vagina?" he deadpanned. "Not a pretty picture either, like the inside of a giant worm's mouth."

I scoffed. "My vagina is fucking beautiful, thank you very much!" And scorching. Very much so.

Callum gave a dry laugh, shaking his head. "I can feel your heat even from here."

My head snapped up, and I shot him a scathing glare. "Get out of my head!"

But Callum ignored me, stepping into a fresh pair of boxer shorts. "You're curious, Savannah," he teased. "You can admit it. It's natural. How do you think you were even conceived?"

"First off, no. I do *not* need a visualization of my parents having sex!" I spat. "And second off, what the actual fuck?"

"Exactly," Callum said. "What the actual *fuck*!"

Laughter bubbled up inside of me, so much so that I could barely contain it. I swore he would be the death of me. If death by laughter was even a thing.

That was one thing Trevor never understood, my strange sense of humor. Because I could joke about sex and the like all I wanted, but when the opportunity finally presented itself, I *knew* I would chicken out. And Trevor always wanted *more*. More kissing, more touching, more *everything*, and even though I was still a virgin, there had always been that expectation that we'd eventually have sex and it would be this magical thing where rainbows rained down on us and unicorns pranced along to the rhythm of our hips.

And that was why we could *never* go back to being just friends. But with Callum, there wasn't that expectation. With him, I could just exist, morbid sex jokes and all.

Speaking of the devil...

Callum pulled his lips into a frown. "At some point when we're not dealing with so much, I *need* to teach you how to close your mind off. This isn't fair to you."

"Why?" I questioned. "What's the point of one more person knowing about my sad existence?"

"There's nothing sad about you, Savannah."

And I didn't know why, but my heart practically bloomed to a seemingly impossible size, and I felt the truth to his words, his love for me despite not being *in* love yet, the sadness he felt whenever I cut myself down.

"And for the record, I can't promise unicorns, but I *could* tape some wooden horns to the foreheads of some wolves, if you'd like," Callum retorted.

And just like that, the serious moment shattered, and my lips pulled into a grin of their own accord. "Just what I need!" I chimed in. "A fake-unicorn audience for when I finally cash in my V-card!"

Callum playfully rolled his eyes. "For a modest human, you certainly *don't* have a modest sense of humor."

I shrugged. "Am I supposed to?"

Callum took a step forward and then another and another until only inches rested between us. "No." And then, he captured my lips in his, and it was like an explosion of butterflies went off in my head, fingers curling at the nape of my neck as he drew me closer so I was flush against him.

My back arched as he nipped at my bottom lip, the friction between us both too much and not enough at the same time. My hands slipped under his shirt, palms gently grazing against skin up, up, up until the shirt was bunched halfway up his torso, exposing the bottoms of firm pecs.

Callum abruptly broke the kiss, gazing at me with serious eyes. "Slow, Savannah. We're going slow."

A soft whine escaped my lips because even though my rational mind was egging me to think about what I was doing, my body wanted to go as fast as humanly possible. And it seemed his did as well, responding in kind to our close proximity with a prodding bulge in his pants.

I gasped as he led me to my bed, gently setting me down as he dropped a short, chaste kiss to my collarbone. And then, he took a few steps back, leaving me feeling cold and empty.

There was a flash of pain in his expression, there one second and gone the next. "Gods, you're so beautiful," he breathed, "but we can't. Not yet."

"Why?" I whined like a child who didn't get their way. My body certainly *felt* ready, so I didn't understand why he was holding back.

A sad smile curved his lips upward. "It's not the right time," he said as if it was the simplest thing ever. "Gods, Savannah, you have no idea how much I want this."

"Then, why did you stop?" I questioned, confused.

"Because you're clearly *not* ready," Callum said, the smile vanishing. "I can sense your indecisiveness, the disconnect between your body and mind. You're not ready, Savannah, and I'm not going to force you into something you may regret later!"

I didn't know why those words affected me the way they did, but in that moment, my heart felt so full I felt like it was ready to burst. *He cares about you,* my mind whispered to me. Finding a man who actually cared about my needs on top of theirs was rare, something not even Trevor was able to do. And Trevor had been my best friend for years.

Had, the same voice said. *Past tense.* He wasn't anymore.

"I need to talk to you about something anyway," Callum said, chasing all thoughts about what could've happened from my mind as the environment dramatically shifted.

Gone was the warmth I had felt, replaced by a dreary cold strong enough to sniff out the remaining light in my world. Whatever Callum had to say must've been important, and for a painful second, I feared he was going to tell me he couldn't keep doing this, that this was a mistake. That *I* was a mistake.

Instead, what he actually had to say was much worse. "I don't think we should look for a way to break the curse anymore."

And just like that, the tiny sliver of balance I had found shattered into a million tiny pieces. "You said you'd help me," I said quietly before screaming, "You *promised*!"

"I know, but that was before," Callum said.

The blood in my veins froze. "What do you mean?"

Callum held his hands out to the side. "One of the witches was here. I ran into her during my run," he said. "She *threatened* us, Savannah! She threatened *you*!"

A normal human response to what Callum was saying would've been confusion, followed closely by fear. Fear was natural and healthy, driven by our base instinct to survive no matter what. But fear wasn't what *I* felt after the initial wave of confusion. Instead, a tidal wave of anger slammed into me until all I saw was red. Red, red, red. And at the center of it all was the boy who had simultaneously managed to rebuild my whole world only to destroy it a second time.

I saw the concern for me in his eyes. But if he was truly concerned, then he should understand why I *had* to do this. I *had* to put an end to the curse because it had already taken too much away from all of us. It was time we put our own animosities and grudges aside and stepped forward into a brighter future.

It was what my brother would've wanted, as well as every other person who had lost their lives. I was sure of it, surer than I had ever been of anything else in my life.

Callum's concern soon turned into shock, presumably

when he realized the expression I wore was not something he had been expecting. But by now, he should've known better. He should've known *me* better, if this whole fated mate business came into play.

"I will not abandon my brother *or* my village," I said coldly.

Callum shook his head, determination flashing within his eyes. "But the witch—"

"I don't give a fuck what the witch said!" I snapped. "If you truly care about me, then you would understand why I *have* to do this, with or without your help!"

Callum opened his mouth, presumably about to lodge another protest my way. But then as if thinking better of it, he closed it, defeat radiating off him in waves. "I *do* understand. But Savannah—"

"No *buts*!" I was done with this conversation. He had no right to tell me what to do, absolutely no *right* to take back what he had already promised me. Unless, of course, everything these past couple of weeks had been a lie.

Callum looked pained, and I instantly knew he was reading my thoughts again. "Savannah, no! That's not—"

"Then, tell me, Callum! Tell me why the sudden change!" At this point, tears pooled in my eyes, and I let them fall, each one dedicated to someone who had lost their life. I even shed some for those who were cursed, whomever they may be, because they were also victims in all this. Victims that would also have to lose their lives for the good of the rest of the village.

I never thought of myself a killer until now except when it came to the beast. But now, I would be forced to end human life in order to save everybody else.

Callum shook his head, his own tears glistening in his eyes. "I want...no, I *need* you to be safe," he cried. "If I let them hurt you, I'd never forgive myself."

I wished he hadn't said that, because now, I felt my own pain. I felt the anguish I was clearly putting him through, a girl he had fallen for who clearly had a death wish. A girl who was broken, unable to be fixed, always ticking the same sad tune. I wanted to yell, to put as much distance between us as possible as if the tether that held us together would suddenly snap, and we'd both be free.

But something told me that would hurt even worse. I let out a sob, realizing we had been doomed from the start, two people who came from completely different worlds. Him from a world of creation, and me one of destruction.

And I was not done with my path yet. For me, the journey has just begun, and I would see it through whether Callum came with me or not.

Callum must've sensed that I wasn't going to budge, because he closed the gap between us so quickly, I suddenly found it hard to breathe. "I'm sorry," he said softly. "I'll still be with you, one hundred percent. Despite what the witches may do."

And then, he kissed me with more passion than I had ever felt before, as if making his promise official. As if sealing the deal, him deciding to finally fully cross over to my world of darkness where neither one of us would come out the same.

My head was spinning, ready to burst with every single heavy sensation my body was going through. Callum's woodsy scent surrounded me, his taste sweeter than honey as he dipped his tongue into my mouth. It was as if I had been starved of oxygen for way too long, finally able to breathe once again as our tongues moved in a synchronized dance.

And I was sure if I looked up, rainbows would be raining down on us as we lost ourselves to the moment, my heart beating in tune to his own.

I blinked at him when we finally broke the kiss, already feeling starved at the loss of contact. "Take me," I breathed as need pulsed between my legs.

Callum seemed to sense a shift in me because he nodded before repeating, "Slow, Savannah."

Slow. There was that damn word again, a word meant to keep me from reaching what I truly wanted. I understood why he was doing what he did, though. He wanted to ease me into it, ease me into this new experience with the hope I would swim instead of flounder.

"You're still not ready. At least, not ready for the main event," Callum said, to which I whined in protest. He held a single finger up, and I immediately quieted. "But there's still more I can do. On the bed."

I didn't know why, but I did what he said without any question, the throbbing becoming almost painful. Callum descended on me, his eyes roving over my form like a vulture about to devour its prey.

"Top off," Callum commanded, reaching for the bottom of my shirt. With his help, I managed to pull it over my head and toss it onto the ground. Yet when I reached for the button on my jeans, Callum shot his hand out, stopping me. "Not yet."

I opened my mouth to protest, but before any words came out, Callum climbed on top of me, pinning my body down with the heat of his own. The friction between his bulge and my throbbing core was almost too much to handle, even with the clothing separating us.

Callum ripped off his shirt before peeling away my bra, and within moments, my breasts tumbled free, nipples already hardening in his presence. He tossed both articles of clothing away before saying, "Bottoms stay on."

"Why?" I questioned, but I never got an answer, for in an instant, Callum climbed lower, his hot breath fanning over my skin before taking one of my hardened nipples in between his teeth.

I let out a gasp, my hips bucking as he sucked, rolling the sensitive bud across his tongue. My thighs clenched around his waist, trying to force him to claim all of me, but he didn't budge, instead continuing his slow, torturous caress of my breast.

Callum's hand trailed down between my legs, stroking my folds through the fabric, as he moved his mouth to my other breast, prodding, sucking, biting until I was nothing more than a puddle as my body shuddered underneath him.

Callum took up the pace, rubbing faster and harder as I moved closer and closer to the edge. "So needy," he moaned into my flesh, tongue flicking the nipple back and forth as if in a game of ping pong.

"Callum, please," I panted. I was close, closer than I had ever been before, and it was definitely something I was *not* used to. I had never been so turned on in my life. Until now, I didn't even think I was *capable* of being turned on in such a manner. He was the first man I had ever felt this budding attraction towards, and I hated to admit a part of me was scared. Because I was a woman who always liked being in control, and I hated being lost to the sensations Callum was delivering to me.

But at the same time, I was surprised to find I actually *liked* it. I liked being taken care of in such a delicate manner by a man who seemed to know my body's needs better than I did. A part of me knew it was because of the mate bond. Because of that, he would always know what I needed, and right now, he was finally delivering, even if our bottoms were still on.

And when I finally climaxed, a shudder wracked my entire body as my hips slammed into his waiting hand, something akin to a scream pouring from my mouth. But I wasn't in pain. In fact, I was far from it as wave after wave of pleasure slammed into me at full force, leaving my head a spinning mess. *How the fuck is this possible?* I wondered, riding my orgasm as if it would be the last one.

Callum detached his mouth from my breast with a faint popping sound before climbing further up my body. "Relax," he commanded, capturing my mouth with his once again as he eased me down from my high until I was no longer floating in the clouds.

And I was left feeling more satisfied than I had ever felt before.

~*~

"So, why do you refer to it as *your* wolf?" I questioned Callum a little over a week later. The two of us were currently cooped up in the attic, enjoying a lunch of turkey sandwiches, potato chips, and lemonade I had prepared myself.

Ever since the day Callum had given me my first ever orgasm, the two of us had grown even closer than we did before. Despite the small fight we had had, he never once brought up us abandoning the curse again and instead resorted to helping me like before. Though despite that, we still came up with nothing as he sniffed even more humans in his wolf form.

I hated to admit how disappointed I was because with the next full moon only mere days away, we were running out of time. And we still had no lead other than Trevor.

And I wasn't yet ready to accept his family may be cursed.

Callum stilled at my question, his sandwich halfway to

his lips. "What do you mean?"

"You know what I mean. Why do you say, 'my wolf'?" I repeated, leaning forward. He had only said this to me a few times, but this question was still burning a hole through my mind, itching for an answer. "As if you're two separate entities. Aren't you one and the same?"

Callum shrugged, taking a hefty bite of sandwich. "Yes and no," he said. "It's complicated."

"It's weird," I said. "Does your wolfish side refer to you as 'my human'?"

At that, Callum nearly choked. "No! That would be really—"

"Weird, right?" I grinned. "Like referring to yourself in the third person. Could you even imagine? 'My human doesn't much like raw meat, but that's because his tastebuds are too uncivilized to appreciate the delicious sensation of a rare steak.'"

Callum snorted, forced to put his sandwich down. "Oddly enough, that doesn't happen."

"You still didn't answer my question."

Callum shook his head. "Like I said, it's complicated."

I flopped down on my back, my head mere inches from his sandwich. "Enlighten the ignorant human then."

Callum shook his head and snorted. "For one thing, unlike humans and witches, shifters were born with two souls, one human and one animal. These souls were in a sense merged together. So we *are* the same, but at the same time, we're different too."

My eyes nearly bugged out of my head. I couldn't imagine what having two souls was like. I could barely manage having *one.*

"It's because of this where I can sense another consciousness, my wolf—something whose needs differ from my human ones," Callum continued. "Wolves don't understand human concepts, so usually if we feel something that is more wolf than human, we attribute it to being our *wolves* want this or our *wolves* need that. It's like being split down the middle, if that makes sense."

"Strangely, it does," I said. I didn't know why it made sense to me, considering I wasn't a shifter. But for some reason, it did. *Probably the mate bond,* I thought, for the mate bond *had* to be the culprit.

Callum nodded thoughtfully. "Sometimes, we can even *hear* another voice in our mind, that of our wolf. Because we technically have two consciousnesses living inside of us, we are susceptible to hearing two kinds of voices."

"Has anyone ever told you hearing voices is *not* good?" I smirked. "Perhaps you should get that checked out."

For a moment, Callum's face looked like it was made of stone. And then, the widest grin I had ever seen split his lips before a hearty laugh tumbled out once my joke registered. "Typical human," he joked, causing me to smile as well. "Always jumping to conclusions."

I shoved a couple chips into my mouth and chewed thoughtfully. "It's still weird though. Like I can't even imagine."

Callum picked up his sandwich with one hand and ran his fingers through my hair with the other. My scalp tickled with the soft caresses, and I was instantly transported back to the day he took care of me.

We hadn't had another day like it, and I hated to admit how much I needed another session. But Callum was still adamant we take things slow, still convinced I wasn't quite ready for the full thing yet.

I didn't know why he thought that because I *felt* ready. But it seemed he knew something I didn't.

Callum frowned, his hands stilling in my hair. It was another reminder I still couldn't block him from accessing certain thoughts, and I was sure my face turned beet-red. "There would be no going back, Savannah," he said softly, almost sadly. "The reason you feel this way is because of the mate bond."

I had a feeling that was why because I had never felt this horny before, but it all still felt so real. "What's happening to me?" I whispered, not sure if Callum heard me.

"What you're experiencing now is only a sliver of what the bond can do," Callum explained solemnly. "It *needs* sex to be completed in full, which is why you feel the way you do. It's also why I've been abstaining, because it isn't you who truly wants it but the bond."

A slap in the face would've hurt less than what Callum just told me. It explained so much, why he still refused to fill me in the way I thought I needed.

"And past the bond, I can still sense your indecisiveness," Callum continued. "You're still just wetting your feet. You're not ready to complete the bond yet."

This, at least, was true, and if I concentrated hard enough, I could just about break through the sensations the bond was *making* me feel and stumble upon something I knew without a doubt was one hundred percent *me*.

"Thank you for always looking out for me," I said softly. "I don't know if I've ever said that."

"You haven't," Callum said, "but I knew already. And you're welcome."

And for a moment, I didn't need anything else, content enough to be in the same space as my mate. For a moment, I let him massage my scalp as I slowly drifted off, the rest of my lunch forgotten.

TWENTY

CALLUM

The next full moon was only days away, and my wolf was clearly growing anxious. Even though I wasn't a werewolf and could shift whenever I wanted, full moons still affected all supernatural creatures. The magic of witches grew even stronger, and shifters felt a renewed sense of strength that wasn't present on any other day. In fact, the werewolf curse had even been created on the night of a full moon, which was why it was one of the most powerful spells ever created by a witch.

Already, I was starting to feel that renewed sense of strength that would only grow the closer the full moon actually came. But it also meant Savannah and I were running out of time to put a stop to the curse, and fast.

Not a day went by that Sahara's threat played over and over again in my mind, causing doubt to stir in my gut that I made the right decision. Oftentimes, I would question myself, wondering if I should've fought harder to get Savannah to give up this suicide mission, but whenever I read her thoughts and was reminded of how happy and content she was, I knew I made the right choice, witches be damned.

Because despite what Sahara had said, my sentiment still stood. The humans of this small village had suffered long enough, and it was time to set them free. But first, we had to figure out exactly *who* was cursed. The one thing I knew was that it wasn't Savannah or any of her parents, because they all smelled normal to me. Plus, Savannah even admitted before she met me that she had never gotten a full night's sleep, most of it spent hunting for the beast that never showed. It had to be someone or multiple people who *did* sleep the entire night and wouldn't remember the transformation or what they did during it.

In fact, the only person who smelled a little funny was Savannah's ex, Trevor, but the last time I brought that up, she shot me down in a heartbeat. She claimed there was no way it could be him because she had known him for years, and they were at one point very close, but that hardly counted as proof that he *wasn't* cursed. Savannah had never spent a night with him, let alone one during a full moon. If she had, then her argument would hold a little more merit.

"I wonder if it's Ronna or Briana," Savannah mused the day after our lunch date. I was once again in wolf form, strutting beside her like the loyal companion I was, sniffing at everyone we passed.

Who are they? I questioned, curiosity having my ears twitch.

"They were Matilda's friends," she explained. "Ronna had won the archery competition, remember?"

I *did* remember Savannah telling me about it and how she had scored second place, though I hadn't been there myself. At the time, I had still been restrained in my fated mate's attic, still a suspected murderer. Even then, I had been captivated by her, even though I also simultaneously thought she was going to torture me.

What makes you think they're the ones who are cursed? I inquired.

Savannah shrugged. "I don't know." She sighed, her shoulders sagging. "Honestly, I'm grasping at straws at this point. We may not know *until* the full moon."

That was a scary thought, because it meant more people could die before we uncovered the truth. *Let's hope it doesn't come to that,* I said, letting a whine escape my muzzle.

Savannah smiled, patting me on the head. "Such a good and loyal dog!" she chimed.

I growled. *I'm a wolf, not a dog!*

Some people passing us by shot Savannah a concerned look while giving me a wide berth, but Savannah didn't look fazed. "Rex doesn't like being called a dog!" she chirped in her normal carefree manner. "Isn't that right, buddy?"

In response, I whimpered in what I hoped would convince people I was a normal wolf. Normal wolves couldn't understand language aside from a few words here and there, and that was only if they were trained.

Internally, however, I scoffed. *Rex again? Seriously?*

Cool it, Rex, or else I'll have your hide! Savannah laughed, moving her hand to scratch me behind the ear. And *damn* did it feel good, causing me to involuntarily lean into her touch as if I *was* a normal, run-of-the-mill wolf.

"I'll buy you a huge chunk of meat. Would you like that?" Savannah cooed, keeping up the charade.

Most wolf shifters actually don't like raw meat, contrary to popular belief, I told her.

I figured, Savannah said, *considering what you usually choose whenever you raid my fridge.*

I yipped, nudging her side with my snout. *I never said I didn't like raw meat. I actually* am *one of the few who doesn't mind it.*

Savannah shook her head. "One raw, juicy steak coming right up!" And then, she switched directions, pivoting straight to what looked like a quaint, butcher's shop.

By the time she returned with the steak in hand, my mouth was practically watering. It was my wolf's way of telling me how content he was, especially since it was our mate feeding us. Savannah took the steak out of the bag, still glistening with moisture, and threw it on the ground at my feet.

I tore into the meat as if my life depended on it. Admittedly, raw meat tasted a whole lot better when I was *in* wolf form, but it also didn't give me a chance to savor the taste as my wolf swallowed bite after bite. Anyone looking would think I hadn't eaten in weeks, and even Savannah looked somewhat shocked with how fast I was wolfing down the steak.

"You can slow down, you know," she commented. "The steak isn't going anywhere."

So good, a voice purred, one I knew instantly as my wolf. Savannah's eyes shot open wide, and I had no doubt she had also heard my wolf's declaration.

Okay, that was weird, she said. *Like, it sounded like you, but at the same time, it didn't.*

If I were in my human form, I would've laughed. *Welcome to what it's like as a shifter.*

Savannah shook her head. *Well, I'm glad* all *of you is now content, but if you don't mind, once you finish that, we really need to get back to work.*

Mate. Mine, my wolf chimed, and I couldn't help but agree.

Savannah just shook her head and tsked. "Whatever am I going to do with you?"

I finished the meat and pawed at her leg, whining. *You'd be lost without me.*

"Perhaps." Savannah laughed. "Come on. Let's get going." And then, we were off once again to find the source of the curse.

For hours, we trudged through town, but still, I found nothing. Not even Ronna and Briana, two girls we had ran into not even thirty minutes after my treat, had given off a strange scent. And with every person we passed who yielded a dead end, I could tell Savannah was growing more and more anxious.

By the time the sun finally set, we returned to her house with another defeat lingering in our faces. "It's not fair!" Savannah whined the moment we entered her room and I had shifted back. "We should've found something by now!"

I didn't want to remind her that I *had* found something in Trevor for fear of upsetting her further. What I really wanted to do was catch a whiff of Trevor's parents and any other living family members he may have just to make sure, but I knew Savannah would never allow it. Because doing so would be accepting there was a possibility his familial line was the one that was cursed.

So, I pulled on more of Savannah's father's clothes and shook my head. "I know. I'm sorry."

Savannah threw herself onto her bed and heaved a massive sigh, her disappointment practically radiating off her in waves. "No, this is my fault," she said. "My stupid mission."

I took a seat beside her. "Nothing about you is stupid, Savannah."

Savannah let out a bitter laugh. "We could be enjoying our time together, and instead, I'm forcing you to help me chase a ghost."

This caught me by surprise. "You're not forcing me to do anything," I reminded her. "I volunteered, remember?"

"Only because you feel something for me."

"That plays a part, yes." I paused. "But I also feel your village has suffered long enough. I *did* ask the witch to lift the curse, by the way."

Savannah's eyes widened. "You did?"

I nodded slowly, taking one of her hands in my own. My heat instantly mixed with hers, and a sigh came from my wolf.

"What did she say?"

"She refused, and that's when she threatened us," I explained. "Witches are very vengeful creatures. They don't forgive and forget easily."

"But shifters do?" Savannah questioned.

I shook my head. "Not all of them. But I don't think it's right for people to be punished for the mistakes of their ancestors."

Perhaps I had at one point. Perhaps when I was younger, I had viewed all humans as monsters who would destroy my kind if given the chance. But Savannah was proof that good humans *did* exist.

And besides, there were bad people everywhere. Bad shifters existed too. Not all packs were run the same as my pack was. Some had even turned their backs on Alonsia.

Savannah closed her eyes. "Sometimes, I wonder what it would've been like if I hadn't been born here. If I hadn't even been born human."

I stilled. "What do you mean?"

"I wouldn't be as broken. I probably wouldn't have lost a brother I loved more than anything else in the world," Savannah said. "I probably wouldn't have wasted time trying to avenge said brother's death. And a part of me thinks I would've found happiness a lot sooner."

"That may be true," I said, "but the opposite could've also been true. That's why it's not healthy to dwell on what-ifs."

Savannah let out a soft chuckle. "Wise words from a wolf shifter."

"I have my moments." I shot her a smile, giving her hand a light squeeze.

Savannah pushed herself into a sitting position, legs haphazardly thrown across my lap, as she snaked an arm around my shoulders to steady herself. Her hand squeezed mine back, and as her eyes locked onto mine, I knew I was a lost cause. The slightest brush of fingertips skirted down my back, and I nearly groaned, feeling the need course through my veins.

"Make me forget," she whispered, leaning her head against the crook of my neck. "Remind me why I'm here."

I could think of a lot of ways to make her scream my name. I thought of her, bent over the bed, as I drove into her again and again, her hair brushing the soft sheets. But mostly, I thought of what her flesh would taste like as I bit into her shoulder, marking her as *mine* as the bond finally completed.

But I couldn't do any of that to her, at least not yet. Because as I combed through her mind, I always found that one spot, the one not corrupted by the mate bond. And it was that part I held onto as I told her to take it slow again and again.

She wasn't ready, at least not one hundred percent. And though I did what I had to in order to make the pain less bearable, I drew the line at cementing something she wasn't yet fully ready for.

My wolf still didn't understand why I chose to wait. He didn't understand how important consent was or why I was so adamant about it. And if Savannah had been another wolf shifter, we probably *would've* cemented the bond by now.

I untangled myself from her, much to my wolf's chagrin, and placed a delicate finger on her bottom lip. "Slow," I reminded her.

Savannah responded in kind by sucking my finger into her mouth, swirling it around as she tasted every inch. The corners of her lips lifted up in a grin as mischief danced in her eyes.

This girl knew what she was doing to me, and it was getting harder and harder to resist her. My dick twitched just thinking about what she could do with her tongue, and I was mere seconds away from jumping her.

She detached her hand from mine and lightly cupped the bulge in my jeans, thumb stroking over the fabric. I hissed, my entire body shuddering, and I leaned just *that* much closer so I could smell her intoxicating scent, lips mere inches from her collar bone.

No! The thought suddenly slammed into me, and I immediately pushed her away as I shot up from the bed. Hurt blossomed on Savannah's face as I rejected her advances, and for some reason, it made me feel like I kicked a helpless kitten. "We can't do this."

Savannah frowned. "Why? I know you keep saying I'm not ready, but—"

"I want you, more than anything I've ever wanted in the world," I said, taking a careful step towards her. "And someday, I'll show you just how much you mean to me. But you deserve the world, Savannah, where you're the only focus and not a distraction from the full moon!"

Savannah pursed her lips. "You took care of me, so why can't I take care of you?"

Good question, I thought, but I knew why. I only gave her a taste of what she wanted to help relieve the ache, but if she returned the favor, I feared my wolf wouldn't let me stop until we've gone too far. I refused to take her choice away from her, and I *knew* her. From the first time she saw me naked, she even admitted she never felt the need for sex and even seemed somewhat appalled by the idea. But that was weeks ago, and the bond was growing stronger by the day.

And I wanted her first time to be special, not just some quickie used to make her forget about her problems. I wanted to take my time with her, savor every last drop she had to offer, so I could remember every single moment down to the last detail.

I wanted to shower her with love and affection first. Cementing the mate bond was a huge deal, and I wanted it to be as big a spectacle as a human wedding was. Because she deserved nothing less.

But when Savannah blinked at me, I could tell she was a lost cause, the mate bond taking away every last sense of rationality. "I need you," she whined. "Please. I promise to be good."

It seemed I was a slave to her as much as she was a slave to me because my feet started moving towards her of their own accord. "Lean back and spread your thighs," I growled, and I instantly knew it was the voice of my wolf. If I wasn't careful, I knew he'd take over in a heartbeat.

Savannah did as she was told, her growing need slamming into me at full force. I placed my center against her throbbing core, placing both hands on her thighs. "Shirt stays on this time," I growled as I yanked on the waistband of her pants, gently pulling them down. "And I remain fully clothed."

Savannah whined but relented, lifting her butt to give me better access. Quickly, I tore her pants away, my eyes instantly drawn to her already soaked center. Her body was more than ready for me, it seemed, and for a moment, my wolf begged for me to rip everything off and take her without mercy.

But this wasn't about what my wolf wanted. This was about her needs, and right now, she *needed* a quick release.

She *needed* something to take the edge off.

"Hands above your head," I instructed, fingers diving underneath the fabric of her lace panties. "And keep them there or I stop."

Savannah bit her lip but nodded, the slightest bit of tears glistening in her eyes. "Please," she gasped. "I need you. *All* of you."

"I know, baby. I know." Slowly, I slid her underwear down. "I'll take the pain away and make it all better."

This, at least, was a promise I knew I'd be able to keep.

TWENTY-ONE

SAVANNAH

I was starting to think I was a lost cause, an empty vessel that constantly needed to be filled. It wasn't enough that Callum tried to take care of me in the best way he knew how. The bond transformed me into a ravenous being, and no amount of soft touches or caresses would satiate the growing beast inside me.

But when Callum went down on me, practically eating me from the inside out, I felt like I was about to spontaneously combust. My body shuddered as his tongue flicked in and out, teeth lightly scraping my clit with abandonment. "Fucking hell!" I screamed, my veins practically on fire from the pleasure he was milking from my body. "Callum!"

Callum stopped what he was doing, blinking up at me as my pussy wept from the lost contact. "Yes?" he said lazily, a smirk playing on his lips.

"No, don't you dare stop, you tease!" I spat, my thighs clenching around his neck as if to force him back down.

Callum's smirk widened. "What did I tell you about your hands?"

Oh shit! I swore, suddenly realizing my hands were no longer above my head but instead spread across my torso, reaching for the vacant spot Callum had been occupying only a second ago. Hastily, I returned them to their spot above my head, but Callum tsked, clearly not amused.

"What did I tell you about your hands?" he repeated, slowly retreating from between my thighs.

"They're back where they belong now!" I practically cried. "You can't leave me hanging like this!"

"Keep your hands above your head," Callum reminded, "or I stop."

Fuck! My mind practically scolded me for being so stupid. I was close, so unbelievably *close*, and he was going to stop, just like that, because I couldn't keep my damn hands where they belonged.

"Tell you what," Callum said. "I'm feeling quite generous today, so how about we quickly finish you off *without* my mouth this time?"

I would've preferred the mouth, but this was as good as it was going to get, so I nodded vigorously. "Please," I begged, nearly weeping with joy as he moved back to his spot between my thighs.

He lifted his hand so I could see, fingers spreading deliciously apart. And then, he plunged two of them into me with no mercy while his thumb delicately circled my clit. And it was like nothing I had ever felt before. There was no pain, only pleasure as he moved his fingers in and out, in and out in a continuous rhythm.

I felt like I was on the edge of a cliff, and the only one keeping me from falling over the side was Callum as he continued to undo me one plunge at a time. And when it seemed like my body could no longer hold on, when I was nothing more than mesh at the hands of him, he gave one final, deep plunge up to the knuckles.

"Fuck!" I hissed, my body lurching as it emptied its contents all over Callum's hand and the sheets below. Wave after wave spurted out of me, and it was unlike anything I had ever experienced before. I didn't even know it *was* possible for a woman to produce as many sticky, white streams as I did, but once again, I was proven wrong.

Maybe Callum's right, and I'm not broken after all.

Callum slowly retreated his hand, fingers still glistening with my release, as he pulled his lips into a frown. "I *know* I'm right," he said. "You just need a little extra care."

"Okay, we've *got* to talk about you always being in my head," I hissed, my mind still spinning with the high of orgasm.

"And I told you I'd teach you, but—"

"Not while we have so much going on with the curse," I finished. "Yeah, I know." In hindsight, I should've felt elated he chose to focus on one thing first, giving me time to adjust. And to be honest, before dealing with the curse, I didn't think I had it in me to concentrate on supernatural mind tricks.

Callum wiped my release off on his skin, and I didn't think watching him do so as if it were lotion would turn me on as much as it did, but for some reason, I was ready for seconds.

"Ready for more already?" Callum tsked. "This mate bond is *really* doing a number on you."

Heat flooded my cheeks, and I squirmed under his penetrating gaze. "You can't sit here and tell me you don't feel it too!"

"Of course I do. But unlike you, I've had years of training." Callum smirked. "*Resistance* training. Because the bond will try to manipulate the mind to get what it wants, and right now, it wants to feel complete, which is *only* possible when—"

"When we make love and you do your wolfy biting thing or whatever, blah, blah, blah." I sighed. "Things were so much simpler before I met you."

But they weren't better, a strange voice whispered in my subconscious, and I had to agree. I felt more alive, more *human*, when I was with Callum than when I wasn't.

My panties suddenly smacked me in the face, followed by my pants. "Get dressed!" Callum said. "This curse isn't going to fix itself!"

I moaned but quickly did as I was told, and soon, I looked like I did before. Like Callum *hadn't* just eaten me out mere minutes ago.

Callum's eyes raked over my clothed body. "Perfect," he said, extending a hand towards me. "Shall we?"

With no hesitation, I took his hand, and together, we left my quaint bedroom and returned to civilization.

~*~

Unlike the few times before, Callum did *not* shift into his wolf. Instead, he continued pulling me along by the hand as if he had something to prove, which in retrospect, he did. We hadn't really discussed labels yet, but I was pretty sure the constant intimate moments we had only happened in couple territory. I didn't know how much shifter society differed from human society, but at this stage, it had to be a given we were exclusive.

Boyfriend had a nice ring to it, perfectly describing what he was to me. My *boyfriend* was parading me through the village, marking me as his. My *boyfriend* ate me out mere moments before. My *boyfriend* was trying to help me break a centuries-old curse that had taken my brother from me.

I smiled at the thought. And then, I internally recoiled because I never used to be *that* girl. The one who always had to be attached to the hip of someone else.

Slowly, I withdrew my hand from his, and he glanced

back with concern and—dare I say it—hurt. "You okay?"

I shot him what I hoped was a very convincing smile and straight-up lied. "Yeah." And then, I internally cringed, because of course I had forgotten he could tap into my mind whenever he damn well pleased because I still haven't learned how to block him from reading every thought that came through my mind.

Like now. I could tell he was reading me with the way his brows furrowed, the way his lips pulled into a frown. And then, I felt like absolute shit because he *knew* I lied to him.

"I'm sorry," he whispered, so much so that I had to strain to hear him.

I didn't know what I had been expecting, but him apologizing had definitely *not* been in the mix. After all, none of this had been his fault. In fact, if I hadn't shot him in the shoulder with that damn arrow—

"Just let me be sorry!" he hissed, reminding me once again of how he could read my every thought. My heart panged with how absolutely gutted he looked, so unlike the boy who had gone down on me not even an hour ago.

A blush coated my cheeks as I remembered the array of sensations my body had been subjected to. Sensations I had definitely *not* been used to and still wasn't.

Callum shook his head and sighed. "I'm sorry you were launched into all this without any proper preparation," he continued. "I'm sorry I hadn't been much of a help preparing you, especially once I realized what was going on between us. But most of all, I'm sorry I—"

"No. Don't you *dare* finish that sentence!" I seethed. "I'm the one who practically throws myself at you again and again, and if this bond is truly as all-powerful as you claim it is, it seems you're having just as much trouble resisting this *thing* as I am!"

I wanted to scream. I wanted to make the biggest scene imaginable. I wanted to close the gap between us and beat my fists against his chest until he finally saw reason, that even though everything has been happening way too soon and I viewed my body as a traitor most of the time, I didn't regret a single moment. Because this journey I found myself on has been one of the most enlightening journeys I have ever taken. A journey that allowed me to learn much more about myself than I had ever thought possible, among them the fact I *wasn't* as broken as I thought I was. I was just as capable of living to the fullest as anyone else, and *damn* Callum for trying to take that away from me!

Another streak of pain flashed in Callum's eyes. "I just don't want to force you into something you're not ready for."

A wave of fury crashed through me just then. "I have a lot of regrets in my life. Letting my brother die when I could've stopped him is probably my biggest one," I hissed, giving him my best glare. "But you know what I *don't* regret? You. Every moment we have spent together, kissing, *more* than kissing, all of it—I don't regret a single moment, and you know why? Because for the first time ever,

I'm discovering little things about myself I didn't even think were possible, and all this is because of one stubborn wolf shifter who crashed through the walls I meticulously spent *years* building up! And you just, what…want to take all this away as if it meant nothing?" *As if* I *meant nothing*, my traitorous mind added, causing tears to glisten in my eyes. I spent most of my life believing I was nothing, that I was incapable of functioning like a regular person because of how many damn skeletons I had to keep hidden. And there was no damn way I could go back to that, not after being shown the other side of life, the one where maybe I turned out okay in the end.

"Savannah, I…" Callum began but then suddenly stopped, something akin to resignation slamming through the bond. "You're right. I haven't been fair. This is new to me too."

The last part caught me by surprise. "What do you mean?"

"Never in my life did I imagine being mated to a human," Callum said. "I spent my entire life thinking there was something wrong with me too, because *no one* in my pack was my fated. I was starting to think Alonsia didn't think me worthy enough, like that was her way of saying I wasn't *worthy* of being alpha." He paused, his eyes developing a faraway look. "It's no secret I'm finding it harder to live up to the alpha name than my father. If I *also* remained mateless—"

"But you're *not* mateless," I said as if that should've been obvious.

"You think I knew that at the time?" Callum huffed. "I was *ecstatic* when I found out I had a mate! And the last thing I want to do is fuck it up!"

Uncomfortable silence stretched between us with those last words. By that point, he had turned around fully, and we were so close to each other our bodies nearly touched. I should've turned around and ran as fast as I could, but my feet stayed rooted to their spot, my traitorous heart seemingly beating a thousand times per minute.

I was falling for him hard. And I didn't know how to stop.

The guttural sound of a throat clearing in our general vicinity shook the both of us out of whatever spell we had found ourselves in. I froze, the two of us craning our heads towards the sound.

My heart suddenly stopped like a bomb detonating in my chest. Because standing just a few inches from us was Trevor Browning.

And he did *not* look happy.

TWENTY-TWO

CALLUM

I hated this guy more than anyone, and not just because he was Savannah's ex. The guy practically oozed entitlement from his pores, as if he somehow had any sort of claim to the girl currently clutching my hand in a death grip.

As if he owned her. My blood boiled at the mere thought. Because even though my wolf would claim otherwise, Savannah was my equal in every sense of the word. Protectively, I stepped closer to her in order to show this asshat exactly who he was messing with.

Trevor sized me up, and I could practically guess the thoughts churning around in his head. He was determining whether or not he thought he could take me, and he must've decided he would lose because he took a huge step back. "Who's this, Sav?" he demanded.

Beside me, Savannah stiffened. "Trevor, this is Callum," she said, motioning between us as if she were just introducing two of her friends. Which, to her, she probably was. "Callum, Trevor."

It was almost comical to see how ghostly Trevor's skin got when Savannah mentioned my name. He had definitely heard of me before, and judging by his face, he wasn't happy in the least. "Callum?" he repeated, as if testing the name himself. "*This* is the man you were practically screaming for when you were on a date with me?"

Uh oh. My wolf growled low in my chest, itching to tear this guy into shreds. I immediately pulled on the reins, because the last thing I needed was an impromptu shift in public.

Savannah didn't seem the least bit fazed by Trevor's proclamation. "What date?" she spat. "I thought we were going there as friends!"

Trevor let out a bitter laugh. "If that's what you truly believed, you're stupider than I initially thought."

"*Don't* call her stupid!" I snapped. It was getting harder and harder to keep my wolf at bay, and if this asshole said one more damn thing against *my* Savannah—

"Callum," Savannah said softly, delicately placing her free hand on my arm. "It's okay. I got this."

I had no doubt she could handle herself. She proved it

time and time again. And so, despite my wolf's whines, I took a metaphorical step back and gave her the reins.

Savannah took a deep breath. "We. Weren't. Good. Together," she began, punctuating each word. "How many more times am I going to have to say that before it finally registers in your thick skull?"

Trevor balled his hands into fists. "I get it. So, *I'm* not good enough for you, but *he* is? Is that it?" His voice rose in volume with each word, so much so that we were now gathering an audience.

An audience we could *really* do without. "Savannah," I said, trying to steer her away from the spectacle, but she wouldn't budge. And suddenly, I felt bad for Trevor for the whirlwind he had just unleashed.

A whirlwind in the form of blonde hair and blue eyes that was now assessing Trevor as if he were nothing more than the poor building in her wave of destruction. "I tried to be nice, but apparently, nice doesn't work on you, so how about this?" She smirked, actually *smirked*. "You're a *terrible* kisser, you always wanted what I couldn't give you, and whenever I said no, you kept pressuring, constantly making me feel like there was something wrong with me. Shall I continue?"

This was new. Admittedly, I only knew the basics from Savannah's past relationship, but to hear *he* was partially responsible for her low self-esteem was almost too much to bear.

"Don't get me wrong. Our friendship meant the world

to me," Savannah continued. "But there was always an end goal with you, wasn't there? Of course there was. Because apparently, guys and girls can't *just* be friends anymore."

Trevor shook his head, seemingly bewildered. "It's not my fault—"

Savannah laughed. "There you go again, blaming *me*! Because I was stupid and naïve and thought the world of you until I finally decided to pursue what made *me* happy!" Her voice trembled, and I fought the urge to reach out and tug her to my chest. No one had the right to make her feel this inadequate, least of all him.

Trevor narrowed his eyes. "Right, because nothing says happiness quite like revenge."

I couldn't take it anymore, for it became painfully clear this guy wasn't going to get it. Before I realized what was happening, I tore my hand from Savannah's grasp and lunged myself at Trevor with everything I had. The two of us soon crashed to the ground in a flurry of punches and kicks as I fought to put this asshole in his place.

I barely registered Savannah continuously calling my name as I landed punch after punch to Trevor's face, my wolf howling in approval at the violence. I barely registered much of anything except for the boy sprawled out below, trying—but failing—to shield his face from my never-ending blows.

Strong, delicate hands soon clutched my shoulders, and if it weren't for my wolf nuzzling up against my rib cage, I wouldn't have registered the touch as Savannah's. My own mate was trying to pry me off her ex, all the while incoherently screaming.

At least, I *thought* her screaming was incoherent, until my senses started clearing, and I could finally make out what she was saying.

"Callum! Stop! You're going to kill him! Oh god! Are you even listening to me? Callum, *please*!"

The fight in me immediately left upon hearing my mate's frantic screams, and I let her pull me off her broken and bleeding ex and lead me far away from the crowd that had gathered.

The crowd of humans who saw me nearly pummel one of their own to death. *I'm such an idiot!*

"No, you're not," Savannah huffed as she continued to pull me in the direction we came from.

I froze. "How did you…"

Savannah tapped her head with a single finger from her free hand. "The bond, remember?"

"Yeah, but *I* know how to filter out my thoughts!"

Savannah shrugged. "You're in a frenzy, Callum. You're not thinking clearly."

Clearly. I couldn't help but agree. I had never lost control *that* badly before, had never even come *close* to killing someone else before. Some shifters may have seen no harm in giving into their basic, animalistic instincts, but my pack was different. We prided ourselves on remaining in control.

I used to be right there with them, but Savannah wasn't

the only thing the bond was slowly changing. Apparently, it was changing me too, warping me into a person I barely even recognized. And I didn't know what scared me more, the changes the bond was inflicting on me or the fact a part of me *liked* what was happening. A part of me *relished* in these new changes, because apparently, this was exactly what I needed in order to cement my claim as alpha. Apparently, I deserved to be feared for what my wolf and I could do.

Or at least, that was what these changes were telling me.

"Would you've actually killed him?" Savannah asked suddenly, interrupting my thoughts.

I didn't want to lie to her, but at the same time, I didn't want to scare her either. She was quickly becoming my everything, and I was slowly realizing I couldn't go back to the way things were without her. Before I met her, I had been empty, devoid of the one thing shifters needed in order to be full.

I thought Alonsia had forsaken me, and I was glad that didn't seem to be the case.

I must've stayed silent well past the acceptable window for a response because Savannah gave me a small smile and said, "You can be honest. I'm not scared."

I felt the truth to her words through the bond, like a very evident slap in the face. After today, she had every reason to be scared of me, and yet...

"Yes," I said softly as my eyes met her stare, letting

what went unspoken float between us. That his words to her affected me more than I'd like to admit and that I relished in having his life in my hands.

At that point, we both knew that if Savannah hadn't done something, Trevor would be dead. But for some reason, my mate didn't recoil in fear and disgust like I thought she would. Instead, she looked intrigued and a little sad.

My fingers itched to pull her closer to me, to further lose myself to her warmth as I comforted her. And I almost did, until she opened her mouth again.

"Thank you," she said, further proving she was somehow different. Most people wouldn't be thanking someone for almost killing someone else directly in front of them. She blinked slowly as she let go of my hand, skirting her fingers up until they rested on the underside of my upper arm. Her arms then wrapped around that soft spot as she pulled herself closer to me, resting her head on the crook of my neck. "For having my back. Most people don't understand why we had ended things, my mom included."

Her wording caught me by surprise. "The breakup was mutual?"

"At the time, yes." Savannah sighed. "We figured it would be for the best, but somehow between then and now, that...changed." A light chuckle escaped her lips. "It's funny. My mom would lose her shit if she knew I rejected him. She wants us back together for some reason."

"And your dad?" I couldn't help but wonder.

Savannah shrugged. "He just wants me to be happy. My mom does too, but for some reason, she thinks that happiness *is* Trevor." She shook her head. "I think I've mentioned before I've never really experienced a sexual attraction to anyone before. Trevor never forced himself on me, but he didn't fully understand why I was uninterested in sex and did try to pressure me a few times. One of those times, I almost gave in but chickened out at the last minute."

"You weren't ready," I said. "There's nothing wrong with that."

"That's the thing though. Yeah, he backed off as soon as I turned my yes into a no, but I don't think he truly let that go. And I think that was one of the reasons he agreed to the breakup in the first place," Savannah explained. "And now, for some reason, he wants me back, knowing full well I *still* can't give him what he wants."

This conversation was starting to make me feel angry all over again, and for a brief moment, I considered turning around and finishing what I had started.

"Callum, don't," Savannah warned, seeming to sense my newfound anger. "He's not worth it."

It was her words that kept me grounded, her words that stopped me from doing something so unbelievably reckless that I would never forgive myself. Immediately, my anger diminished as I let her lead us back to her house, back to the place where this all started.

And it was only after we returned that I realized we made no progress in discovering who in her village was cursed.

~*~

The day of the full moon started like any other day, aside from Savannah's building anxiety. By this time, I was sure she expected to have already slain the beast, and the fact she hadn't was slowly eating away at her. And I wasn't doing much better, considering I had promised to help her, and all we had to show for our efforts was a dead end.

I wanted to help her still, even now. I wanted to go out there and search around endlessly for the person or people who had been cursed and not stop until I took off their heads, and the only thing stopping me was a promise Savannah forced me to take earlier that morning. That I wouldn't do anything rash. She now thought our best course of action was to wait for the werewolf to come to us, which meant waiting until night fell.

And hoping no one was killed in the process.

I knew this new plan pained her, but there was nothing more we could do. My nose hadn't sniffed a single thing, aside from Trevor's odd scent. A scent I hadn't even smelled last time I ran into him, partially because I was too consumed with rage on how he was treating Savannah. I didn't even *think* to sniff around him again in case I had been wrong before, but now, I'd never know.

My nose never lies, my human subconsciousness told me, but I was now questioning whether or not that was true.

Despite everything, Savannah had seemed so adamant his family *couldn't* be cursed.

But if not him, then I truly had no idea who else it could be.

"Stop overthinking!" Savannah scolded me playfully. We were currently in our signature spots in her attic shortly after having breakfast, both of us stuffed beyond reason. Of course, I had to eat in my wolf form, since Savannah's parents were around, and by then, news had spread to them of their daughter's new pet. A pet they were strangely okay with, since they figured I would help Savannah feel less lonely.

And it turned out they were right, though not in the way they imagined me filling that void. I wanted to laugh at the irony but refrained for Savannah's sake.

"I'm not overthinking," I hissed. "I'm just...thinking!" As soon as those words left my mouth, I realized how dumb they sounded, but I didn't much care.

Savannah rolled her eyes. "Well, stop thinking then!" she amended, tucking her knees beneath her small frame.

"That's physically impossible," I pointed out, to which she burst into laughter.

"You know what I meant," she grumbled, her laughter slowly fizzing out until a frown pulled at her lips. "Everything will work out tonight. You know that, right?"

After everything she had been through, everything the curse had taken from her, I didn't understand how she could still be so calm. It was as if we reversed roles, and suddenly,

I was the one who couldn't think rationally.

"A lot can still go wrong," I told her, for it was the truth. We could be too late, and by then, the werewolf would be long gone, leaving a trail of death in its wake.

Savannah pursed her lips together, deep in thought. "But this time, I actually have a plan. *We* actually have a plan." She paused. "Before, I didn't have that, and I think that was why I failed so many times to stop the beast."

"Because you were looking in the wrong place?" I guessed.

She nodded. "I always hunted *outside* of the village, and on nights of the full moon, by the time I returned…" Her words lodged in her throat, and she choked. "Because I never once considered the beast could be one of the villagers, someone I grew up with."

I nodded. "That makes sense."

"And now, whatever happens…I *know* it will end tonight," Savannah continued with such determination, I couldn't help but admire her further. "I can feel it in my gut."

I wished I shared her confidence, but at least one of us still *had* confidence. A chuckle tumbled from my lips, and I shook my head. "You're one of a kind. You know that, right?"

"Of course I am!" Savannah dramatically flipped her hair behind one shoulder. "I'm Savannah!"

This for some reason made me laugh even harder until tears started pooling in my eyes. Savannah matched my laughter with her own, closing the gap between us as we were lost in our own little world.

And then, she kissed me, slow and delicately, as an array of metaphorical fireworks exploded around us. This kiss wasn't like our previous ones, for it had more fire, more heat, as Savannah crawled onto my lap and wrapped her arms around my neck.

I felt like a lovesick teenager, unable to get enough of her as our tongues tangled together in an endless stream to the point where I couldn't tell where she ended and I began.

Home. She felt like home, and it was the most amazing feeling in the world.

And my only hope for tonight was for her to stay put together because I didn't think I could handle watching her soul shatter once again.

However tonight played out, one thing was for certain. The curse had to end, one way or another, because only through its demise would any of us achieve true peace.

Threats from witches be damned.

TWENTY-THREE

SAVANNAH

I strapped my bow and some arrows across my back, feeling every bit the Huntress I was meant to be. A black hood was pulled over my head, hiding my hair to the best of my ability. Everything I adorned tonight was black, down to even a pair of heavy, black gloves to help me blend into the night.

I had absolutely no idea if any of this would help hide me. For all I knew, werewolves had been blessed with heightened vision during the nighttime. Plus, I would also have to contend with the natural light from the full moon, which meant I would have to stick to predominantly shadows cast by nearby buildings. But wearing what I hoped would help hide me made me feel better, especially since I was going out alone.

Without Callum.

At first, the hulking wolf shifter protested, claiming it was way too dangerous. And he was right, to a certain extent. But his wolf could potentially make things more dangerous for me, considering its snow-white color would stick out like a sore thumb.

In the end, we agreed to a compromise. I would go out alone, and he would shadow a great distance behind me in human form. Callum was weaker as a human, but he could also more easily hide if need be.

"I don't like this," Callum said for what sounded like the billionth time. He was directly behind me on my bed, watching as I got ready for what could very well be my funeral. The two of us came down from the attic hours ago as the evening drew near, and he hadn't moved from that spot during the entire time I had been getting ready.

"You don't have to like it," I said, checking my appearance in the mirror to make sure all the important parts were covered. Like my super-white skin I was convinced could reflect light. Satisfied, I spun around on my heels to face him. "But we agreed this was for the best."

"No, *you* agreed." Callum shook his head. "I still think you would be much better off with me by your side."

"And potentially scare the werewolf away." I snorted. "Besides, it's not like you'll be *that* far behind me."

"I still don't like it," Callum said. "What if something

happens, and I'm not quick enough to save you?"

If I was a woman who wasn't used to taking care of myself, I would've found his sentiments somewhat sweet. The fact he cared enough to try to protect me when seemingly no one else bothered was something that made me feel warm. And fuzzy. Two things I was definitely *not* used to feeling. In fact, those feelings were so strange to me, they were right up there with sexual attraction.

Callum smirked, and I knew right then and there that I had accidentally broadcasted my thoughts to him again. "Warm and fuzzy, huh?" he teased.

Embarrassment flooded my system. "Once this is over, you're teaching me how to close my mind to you."

"I thought that was already a given, but if you *insist...*"

I shook my head, giving him a once-over. "Get dressed."

"I *am* dressed," he said stubbornly.

"You know what I mean!" I sighed, exasperated. "Get dressed in something more easy to hide in!"

"Hey, if you're offering..." Callum cleared his throat. "Joking aside, I can take care of myself, Savannah. I have a wolf on my side, remember? Plus, I prefer wearing something I can easily shed at a moment's notice."

Right. Because he had another form he could fight in, and his shifting literally caused him to shred through clothes.

I pursed my lips. "Is that all you shifters wear? Clothes you can easily shed at a moment's notice?"

"No," Callum deadpanned, his smirk slowly returning. "We just don't wear clothes. Period."

Lovely. Figures my mate would live in a nudist colony.

"I can still hear you!" Callum scowled. "And for your information, clothes are a *human* concept. Nudist colonies are *human* concepts because only *humans* feel the need to cover up."

"What about witches?" I asked sincerely.

Callum opened his mouth. Closed it. Then opened it again. "They tend to be prudish, yes," he finally explained. "But sometimes, they go without if amongst family and very close friends."

Gross. I totally did *not* need a visualization of all these naked women running around, their parts jiggling everywhere for all to see. I had a hard enough time trying to juggle Callum's nakedness.

His very *hardened*, chiseled…

I loudly cleared my throat, shaking thoughts of his nakedness from my mind. I was about to do something very important, and I did *not* need the distraction his abs would provide.

I truly am *hopeless…*

Callum chuckled. "Someday, you'll learn, Savannah, that not everyone grew up the same way you did." He paused, his smirk vanishing. "*Everyone* has parts, and if you saw those parts every day, you wouldn't think twice about them."

I had no doubt there was truth to his words, but right

now, this conversation was giving me the heebie jeebies. "Can we stop talking about this please? I have enough on my plate. I don't need to add impromptu nakedness to my growing list of anxieties."

"Not impromptu, at least for us." Callum shrugged. "And besides. *You* asked."

A human expression came to mind. "Curiosity killed the cat" or something of the like. And right now, I felt its full impact, as if I were that cat and Callum just shot me with an arrow.

How ironic.

I shook my head, struggling to clear my mind to the best of my ability. Tonight was an important night, and I didn't need anything hindering my ability to perform.

I shook my shoulders, trying to relax my body as best as possible. *You've got this,* I told myself. I was one of the best damn archers in Ebonrowe and had even nearly killed a wolf shifter. One measly werewolf should be easy.

I just had to keep my distance and hope luck was on my side.

Piece of cake.

"You ready to go?" I asked Callum, turning my back to the mirror and meeting his gaze. Moonlight already started streaming through my small window, and I couldn't afford to waste any more time.

Callum hopped off the bed. "I've *been* ready," he grumbled, his blatant unhappiness streaming through the bond. He still didn't understand why I had to be alone, not really. I still had a lot to learn, but what I *did* know was his wolf side was more animalistic, something he constantly had to keep under control as if training a new pet. And his wolf right now was showing its protective, loyal nature.

It was something I would have to get used to if I truly wanted to be with him.

I shot him what I hoped would be a reassuring smile. "Great! Wait a few seconds, maybe a minute, okay?" I said. "And if anything comes up, I *will* use the mate bond."

And then, I was off, tiptoeing through the house so as not to disturb my parents. At this time of night, though they weren't asleep yet, they *were* in their room, and the last thing I needed was them hearing me and barging out of their room, demanding to know where I was going on the night of a full moon.

There was an unspoken rule in Ebonrowe, where everyone retired indoors before the sun fully set on nights plagued by the full moon. Because no one truly knew what the beast was or when it would strike. At least, that was what was *supposed* to happen, but there were always stragglers, and those were the people that tended to get killed.

I opened my front door as quietly as possible and slipped through the small crack, and the cold, night air washed over me, as if caressing me, offering me comfort.

As if it knew tonight could very well be my last night of life.

Don't think like that! Callum scolded through the bond.

You're making me even more nervous, and I'm this close to saying fuck it and joining you, whether you want me to or not!

I groaned, but internally, my heart warmed at the gesture. *Sorry!* I shot back. *How about this? We're going to get through this night and win!* I threw in some extra cheer for emphasis, and I could practically feel Callum rolling his eyes.

At least it seemed like he no longer wanted to ruin our plan, though.

I swear, you'll be the death of me, Savannah, Callum relented.

Touché, I replied and then put a clamp on the conversation. Because now, I needed to concentrate, and joking with Callum was *not* concentrating.

For hours, I circled the town, looking for any sign of the beast. By then, Callum had left my house as well, always a constant presence staying a few blocks behind me. Originally, I hadn't wanted him to come along at all, but his constant presence gave me the comfort I desperately needed, and I was glad he was here.

Still no sign, I shot through the bond. The streets were nearly deserted with a few stragglers, like I thought there would be. None of them paid any mind to me, seeming lost in their own worlds.

I wanted to yell at them to get inside immediately. I wanted to curse them out for being so stupid. But I also knew if they were here, the beast would surely come, as if they were bait. As soon as that thought entered my mind, I felt sick, because these were all real people with families and friends and *lives*, and I was viewing them as nothing more than a means to an end.

But I also knew for others to live, a few sacrifices would have to be made. I just had to be quick, hoping I could get there in time to save them.

As if on cue, the first scream sliced through the air like butter, causing shivers to wrack my body. I immediately froze, as did the people around me, as the scream abruptly cut off, plunging us all into fear-filled silence.

And then, chaos ensued as people ran every which way, desperate to get indoors before they became the next victim. "It's the beast!" someone yelled to my left at the same time another to my right cried, "We're all doomed!"

My gut twisted as person after person shoved past me, not bothering to give a second look to the girl dressed in all black carrying her bow and arrows around like they were her lifeforce.

In fact, no one seemed to notice me at all, too consumed with their own fear.

A part of me wanted to curse at them for not being at least *somewhat* concerned, but this actually worked in my favor. Another scream pierced the night air, finally spurring my body into action, and I ran against the crowd in the direction the screams were coming from.

My heart was on overdrive, legs pumping faster than they ever have before, and my lungs *burned* as if they had been lit on fire. But I needed to continue moving, needed to reach the screaming individual before it was too late.

By the time I reached a small clearing at the edge of town, all that was left to indicate someone had been there at all was a very prominent trail of blood that skirted to my right and disappeared into a back alleyway. I stiffened, slowing my steps, as I proceeded to follow the trail of blood to what would more than likely end in my demise.

My gut twisted as nerves wracked my system, my hands immediately pulling my bow free. I knew I was too late to save whoever screamed, but maybe, just *maybe*—

My heart came to a full stop as the sound of smacking and satisfied growls infiltrated my ears. My eyes fought to adjust to the darkness caused by the buildings' shadows, and I nocked my first arrow.

Only to be greeted by not one, not two, but *three* wolf-like creatures, all of them bent over their latest catch, smacking their lips as they savored their latest meal.

Completely oblivious to my presence.

I can do this, I thought, aiming my arrow to the werewolf closest to me. And then, I let it fly, watching as it pierced the creature through the gut.

The werewolf howled in pain as it stood on hind legs, whirling around to face me. Just by looking at the bleeding wound, I knew it wasn't a fatal shot, but if I could just—

Something soon slammed into me from the right, causing me to drop my bow as my back slammed against a nearby wall, nearly knocking the wind out of me. I gasped before a burning sensation engulfed my arm, the werewolf who had me pinned digging its claws into my flesh and dragging downwards.

I kicked outwards, my foot making contact with the beast's underside, allowing me a small window of escape. The werewolf howled as I ducked under its arms, clutching my bleeding arm to my chest.

I made a break for my bow, nearly diving for it, before another werewolf was upon me, claws digging into my shoulder before more pain flooded my body. I screamed as the beast's hulking body pinned me down, sending out a short prayer to whoever would listen.

Gods, fuck, I'm going to die!

The werewolf hovered over me, jaws descending downwards to clamp over my neck. Yet, before it could do so, something slammed into its side, knocking it off me in one fellow swoop.

I barely had time to comprehend what was happening as I lunged for my bow again, black spots dancing across my vision. With shaking fingers, I latched onto the hilt and pulled it towards me before whirling around.

Only to find the three werewolves surrounding a magnificent white wolf whose teeth were barred in warning. *Callum!*

I wanted to cry. I wanted to scream. But mostly, I wanted to bury my face into his white fur and sob while he comforted me. Because if I had my way tonight, I would've died. If Callum hadn't been shadowing me, the werewolves would be feasting on me right about now.

I nocked another arrow, fighting against the wave of unconsciousness that threatened to pull me under, just as the werewolves lunged at Callum with claws outstretched.

No! I shouted through the bond, shooting arrow after arrow at Callum's attackers, hoping they hit their mark. Callum effortlessly evaded their attacks, jaws sinking into the werewolf nearest to him.

Callum shook his head, shaking the werewolf around like a ragdoll to disorient it, before dropping it to the ground. And then, he bit into its neck, chomping through skin and bone, before the werewolf finally succumbed to its fate.

The remaining two werewolves howled at their fallen companion before barring their teeth. And then, they ran at Callum with claws outstretched, ready to end him once and for all.

I let loose another arrow, this one sailing overhead to pierce the skull of one of the attackers. It went down in a heap of brown fur, stilling as it made contact with the pavement. I shot one more arrow into where I presumed its heart would be, blood mixing with the fur as it flowed out in endless streams.

I didn't get to relish in my kill, for in that instant, the remaining werewolf threw itself onto Callum's back, claws going right for the throat. *Fuck!* I hissed through the bond as Callum fought to shake off his attacker.

I nocked one more arrow, aimed it at the werewolf's head. *Just one more shot, Savannah, so Callum can finish it off,*

I thought. And then, I let it fly, soaring right for the meaty spot in between the werewolf's eyes.

The creature turned at the last minute, the arrow lightly grazing the side of its face before embedding into its shoulder. The beast let out a howl of pain as it loosened its grip around Callum's throat.

My shot wasn't a fatal one, but that didn't matter once Callum successfully bucked the werewolf off his back and spun around, lips pulled back in warning. And then, he went for the final kill, tearing into the werewolf's throat as if his life depended on it. The creature slackened in Callum's hold before finally stilling, eyes glazing over as its chest gave one final lurch of breath.

And then, Callum let the creature go, its body shuddering as bones twisted and contorted, jutting out every which way. *Holy fuck! It's shifting!* I quickly realized.

Not soon afterwards, the other two carcasses started shuttering in the exact same fashion, and I was forced to watch as fur retracted back into skin and limbs shortened into a natural, human length. Clothing reappeared on each of the human bodies as if by magic.

Apparently, unlike shifters, werewolves didn't shred through their clothing when they shifted. Instead, the clothing magically disappeared, only to reappear once the cursed shifted back.

Interesting. Though I supposed if I were a witch, I'd want to put any precautions I had into place to keep people from suspecting what was really going on. Continuous shredded clothes would've warranted too many questions, leading us to eventually figuring out what was happening on our own.

The black spots swirling in my vision intensified, but I needed to know who the cursed had been, who Callum and I had just killed. As best as I could, I fought against the pain and my growing unconsciousness just in time to see the first lifeless face I recognized.

My heart nearly stopped. It was Trevor's paternal aunt.

Shock ripped my heart in two as his father came next followed by him, the last werewolf to have died by our hands. A lump formed in my gut at this realization, at the fact Callum had been right.

He said Trevor smelled funny, but I had brushed him off because it couldn't be true. Trevor couldn't be cursed, not when I had spent as much time with him as I did.

But the truth was there, practically slapping me across the face, and suddenly, I couldn't feel anything anymore.

"Savannah?" Callum called. He must've shifted back, but even his voice sounded far away, as if we were on opposite sides of a tunnel. "Savannah, can you hear me?"

I tried to nod, but I couldn't move my head. I tried to speak, but my lips remained frozen. Lastly, I tried to move, tried to place one foot in front of the other, but nothing happened. I was a prisoner in my own body, forced to live in my own personal hellscape where my second best friend and first ever boyfriend turned out to be the one behind my village's suffering along with his father and aunt.

Eventually, the pain became too much as my physical wounds broke through the numbness, mixing with the pain in my heart. I couldn't hold on anymore, feeling myself slip closer and closer to oblivion.

Even Callum's voice started fading away as black consumed my vision, and I was out like a lightbulb, barely registering the shock as my body made contact with the ground below.

TWENTY-FOUR

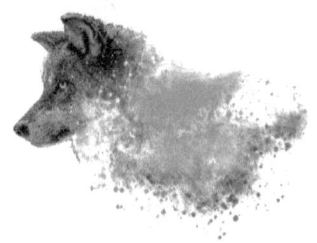

CALLUM

There was still blood on me when I shifted back, but most of it wasn't mine. Searing pain still engulfed my shoulders from when the werewolf latched onto my back and refused to let go. But for the most part, I was okay. Still hyped up on adrenaline, but okay nonetheless.

I couldn't say the same for Savannah.

The poor girl finally succumbed to the shock her frail, human body had been subjected to, the expression she wore as she gazed at Trevor's blank expression still engraved in my mind. I hardly even wanted to believe it myself, but the evidence was right in front of me. That and now I was finally able to discern why he had smelled strange that one day.

All this time, his family had been the ones living with the curse, unbeknownst to them. I may have hated the guy, but I didn't want *this*. I didn't want his family to be the reason Savannah's brother and countless others lay dead because I knew how close he and Savannah had been at one point. If the roles had been reversed and it turned out Sammy, unbeknownst to him, had been killing my people, I wouldn't know what to do.

And Trevor, to have been cursed in such a manner, had succumbed to a fate worse than death, and Sahara's coven was directly responsible. I had almost taken the witch's threats to heart, but now, I was glad I didn't. Because for what the witches had put my mate through, there would be hell to pay.

My discarded clothes laid only a few feet back, and as I retrieved them and slipped them on, all I could think about was how cold my heart felt. My pack may have at one point been allied with the Witches of Old, but that would no longer be the case, if I had anything to say about it.

Remember what the humans had once done to your kind, a traitorous voice whispered deep in my subconscious. And I *did* remember, through history lessons and text documents by shifters everywhere. But there was a fine line between knowing what happened and dwelling on it, and it seemed the witches had crossed that line ages ago.

Slowly, I approached Savannah and took her into my

arms. Her breathing was weak, labored, and she had lost a lot of blood. But she was alive, which was the only thing that mattered to my wolf. "It's going to be okay," I whispered to her, unsure if she could hear me or not. And then, I set off towards the heart of town, hoping to come across a building resembling one of the human infirmaries I've heard about but never visited. *It will be a big building, one of the biggest in the village,* I thought, remembering my human studies from years ago. *Big building...right. Can't miss it.*

What I hadn't anticipated on, however, was how many buildings fit the description of *big.* My shoulders tensed with each one I passed, daring the slightest peek inside as if I could somehow see beds or equipment or *something* that would tell me if I had the right place.

Instead, all I got were dark, empty spaces and a lot of disappointment. *Fuck!*

I was close to screaming, because if I didn't find the infirmary soon, Savannah may not make it through the night. And I'd be damned if I lost my mate this close to finding her.

Deep breaths, Callum. You'll find it.

I must've stumbled through town for a good ten or so minutes before I finally stumbled upon a building that *may* have worked. The lights were at least on, indicating that someone was in there, which was as good a sign as it was going to get.

I rushed towards the building, arms soaked with

Savannah's blood, before practically kicking the doors down and throwing myself inside. "Help!" I screamed, my voice hoarse. "Someone please!"

The sharp click of heels suddenly drew my attention, and a woman about my mom's age appeared, brows furrowed in confusion. She opened her mouth to speak, presumably to ask what was going on, but when her eyes landed on Savannah, her face paled, and recognition dawned on her features. "You better follow me," she said. And then, she spun around to lead me further into the bowels from whence she came.

"It's okay," I kept saying to my mate over and over again in order to convince myself as much as her. "You'll be okay. The nice woman will take care of you."

After a few minutes of walking, the woman led me to a room full of empty beds and IV hooks and a bunch of other stuff I once knew the name of but now couldn't place. My heart nearly wept at having taken that chance and finding the right place as the woman motioned towards one of the beds closest to where we came from. "What happened?"

I carefully placed Savannah on the bed, moving her hair from her face before taking a step back. "The beast," I said, remembering that had been Ebonrowe's name for the curse. "It came out of nowhere."

The woman's eyes nearly bugged out of her skull. "How the hell are you two still alive?"

I didn't have an answer for her, at least none I could tell her. "Do you think you can save her?"

"I'm not going to lie. The wounds are very deep, and it looks like she lost a lot of blood." The woman paused. "However, I think I can do it. It may take several days, but I've seen and treated worse."

I didn't realize how desperately I needed to hear those words, that after everything, my Savannah would be okay. She managed to somehow stare death in the face and merge out on top.

I reached out a delicate finger and traced her jaw, my heart beating in tune to hers. "See, I told you it would be okay." I smiled.

She didn't smile back.

~*~

The first day of Savannah's recovery, I returned to her bedside, my heart sinking when I saw she had not yet awoken. Her wounds had been stitched up and wrapped in bandages, and a couple IV needles were stuck in her arm, feeding her fluids and blood. Her chest rose and fell with the promise of breath, and color had returned to her cheeks.

But the bond still remained silent, the only thing I could gleam from it the fact she was still alive. I held onto that small sliver of the bond as if my entire life depended on it, tears pooling in my eyes that I couldn't just blink away.

"Savannah, if you can hear me," I began, my voice shuddering, "I want you to know how much you mean to me. And I want to remind you to keep fighting. I'm not ready to let you go just yet."

I reached out, clutching one of her hands in my own and delicately stroking the skin. Her hand felt warmer than it did last night, causing the first of the tears to dampen my cheeks as I wept with joy. I cried and cried and cried as silently as I could while still holding her hand, and only when I was fresh out of tears did I finally let go, watching her hand fall back to her side.

And then, I left with the promise to return tomorrow.

~*~

On the second day of Savannah's recovery, the IV needles were gone. A nurse was at her side, a different woman than the one two nights ago, quickly checking her vital signs while forcing some water down her throat. Her face was stoic, betraying nothing, which I took as a good sign. Because if anything *was* amiss, surely her face would show it.

She glanced up at me as I approached. "Callum, is it?" she questioned.

I nodded. "Yes, ma'am."

The nurse shot me a small smile. "Her vitals check out," she said. "She's a fighter, that's for damn sure."

"I wouldn't expect anything less," I told her, and I meant every word. From the first time I met her, I could sense her strength even through her fury. And somehow, I knew she was a woman who couldn't be killed off that easily.

The nurse pursed her lips together. "You know, her parents came by earlier. They asked about you and told me to give you their thanks for saving their daughter's life," she said. "They seemed very grateful. You did good, Callum, whether you believe that or not."

I never met Savannah's parents in my human form, but for some reason, their approval meant the world to me. "Thank you," I said as the nurse moved to skirt right by me. "What's your name?"

The nurse paused and glanced at me with a knowing look. "Sahara," she said, giving me a wink before sauntering out of the room.

My blood froze.

~*~

Another nurse was at Savannah's bedside the third day I came to visit. She stiffened at my approach but didn't tear her attention away from changing my mate's bandages.

"Sahara again?" I practically spat. "Or is it Willow this time?"

The nurse blinked up at me, evidently confused. "Excuse me?"

"You heard me," I growled. If one of those witches came close to her again—

"Sir, I don't know what you're talking about, but I'm going to have to ask you to leave," the nurse said sternly.

I belted out a laugh. "Like hell, I will."

The nurse shook her head, evidently bewildered. "It's Bethany, by the way," she grumbled. "Now, get out before I call security!"

The truth in her words slammed into me, practically throwing me off balance. *Fucking hell!* I cursed, bolting out of there as fast as I could. Because the last thing I needed was to attract human attention.

My mind was a whirlwind of thoughts as I spilled out onto the streets. The witches knew. And now, they were targeting Savannah, my mate, messing with me so I made an absolute fool of myself. I knew I didn't imagine yesterday. Sahara had been *here*, in a different form from when I ran into her in the woods. Checking on her. Spying on us. Presumably investigating the death of the curse.

I balled my hands into fists. I'd be damned if they touched a single hair on her head, especially when she was unconscious and unable to defend herself. The moment she woke, I would take her far away from here to people who could protect her. To my pack.

And damn anyone who got in my way.

~*~

On the fourth day, Savannah's bandages were gone, though the stitches were still there. She was alone, sitting up in bed as she silently ate a sandwich that had been given to her for lunch.

Alive. Awake. Almost healed.

My wolf stirred in my gut as I practically ran to her bedside, yelling, "Savannah!"

She startled as her eyes met mine, and it was as if a storm of emotions crashed into her. Her lips twitched, breaking out into a smile, as she set her half-empty tray down beside her.

I didn't care how I looked as I flung myself into her waiting arms. All I cared about was her, her closeness, the way her body felt against mine, her breath skirting down my sensitive skin, leaving a trail of goosebumps behind. I wrapped my arms around her back, careful not to tear her stitches, as my lips met hers.

I was a beast, starved for too long without her that I barely even lived. The mate bond was a fierce thing, tying us closer and closer together that even though we hadn't cemented it yet, I knew I would die without her. If she had been ripped away from me, I knew I would never recover.

Her lips parted, tongue skirting over my own as her hands slid down my back, squeezing the skin just above the waistband of my shorts. She pulled me closer to her, practically devouring me from the inside out, before I finally pulled away.

"Slow," I purred, stilling a single finger on her lips as she whined in protest. It seemed she had been just as starved as me, but if we didn't slow down, we risked reopening her wounds, and I couldn't allow that to happen.

Realization soon dawned on her features, and she gave a curt nod. "Later then," she said. "What'd I miss?"

I shrugged. "Nothing much. Just a whole lotta grief and neediness, stuff unbecoming of a future alpha." I chose in that moment to leave Sahara's visit out of it for now. Savannah was still recovering, and the last thing I wanted was to upset her.

Savannah chuckled, reaching for her sandwich. "Some things never change, do they?"

I laughed right along with her. "No, they don't."

She stopped, her eyes landing on her sandwich as if in thought. "Is it true?" she questioned, a hint of sadness coating her words. "Was Trevor really—"

"Later. We'll speak later," I said as her sorrow and grief leaked through the bond. "Right now, I need you to focus on recovering. Can you do that for me?"

Savannah shot me a smile, though it didn't quite reach her eyes. "Of course."

And then, she took a hefty bite of sandwich, and all was temporarily forgotten.

TWENTY-FIVE

SAVANNAH

Four days later, the infirmary finally removed my stitches. That was also when I was deemed as fully recovered and could leave whenever I wanted. My parents were the ones to take me home, weirdly scolding me for being so stupid but at the same time expressing how happy they were to see me. I barely registered what they were saying, giving quick nods and short answers when appropriate, but my mind was elsewhere, high up in the clouds where only I could find it.

A pang of disappointment exploded in my gut. Because even though I loved my parents deeply, they weren't

Callum. He had visited me every single day of my recovery, and I hadn't realized how much I needed his company until now. Without it, I may not have come out of this okay.

My parents led me into the house, cooked my favorite meal of spaghetti with a side of garlic bread for lunch, and told me over and over again of how stupid I was and that they *knew* I snuck out of the house every night, because parents for some reason always know, and that this had to end. They told me they had let it slide because everyone grieves differently and I hadn't been hurt before, but now, I could've died, and then, they would've been left having to grieve the deaths of both their children.

Little did they know the beast—or *beasts*—would never plague Ebonrowe again. Callum and I made sure of that.

Trevor's body and his father and aunt had been found the next day after the full moon, and though they didn't sport the usual wounds all victims of the beast had, the town chalked them up to being the latest victims. A part of me still felt sad upon hearing it wasn't all just a dream, that Trevor's family had been the cursed ones all this time, and over the course of my recovery, I grieved the friend I had lost. Even if we could've never gone back to being just friends, I still cared about him.

"Savannah?" my mother suddenly said. "What's wrong, honey? What are you thinking about?"

Tears sprung into my eyes, but I quickly blinked them away. "Trevor," I said honestly, my breath hitching on his name. I had already shed an abysmal amount of tears over his death, but for some reason, there was still more my body had to give.

My mother's expression broke. "Oh, honey," she said, reaching over to hug me in a tight embrace. "I'm so sorry. This world is too cruel."

I knew that up until Trevor's death, my mom still held to the fantasy that we would get back together and everything would be just peachy and that her hug meant more to her than just my ex-best friend dying. But there was something, some hidden comfort, only the affection of a mother could provide, and so, I let her hold me, comforting me as my body shuddered with more sobs than it should be capable of holding. Because now, I had lost two people to the beast.

Mathias and Trevor. Two people who had at one point meant the world to me.

You still have Callum, a voice deep in my subconscious whispered, causing my heart to flutter. A small smile spread across my lips, because that meant not all hope was lost. I hadn't lost *everything*, for I still had my parents and Callum.

My mom broke the embrace, and then, we returned to our meal. Once we were finished, plates were cleared and washed, and I managed to escape under the guise I needed some privacy.

What I really needed, however, was to see my mate, for him to hold me as he devoured me with kisses and the promise of a brighter future. One that could only go up from here now that the curse was no more.

I hoped he would still be here by the time I got out of the infirmary, that he hadn't left yet to go back to his pack. And I didn't know if that was more wishful thinking on my part because I *knew* he had other responsibilities as the future alpha, ones he had neglected for way too long to help me.

But as I stumbled up the stairwell and yanked open the door to the attic, my heart blossomed as my eyes met the waiting gaze of my mate.

He was still here, seated on the attic floor near the restraints I had originally had him in with a huge smile on his face. His arms spread wide, beckoning for me to leap into them without a care in the world.

And that was exactly what I did, practically scrambling up the rest of the way before slamming the door shut behind me and crawling towards him. I reached for him, and he met me halfway, pulling me up onto his lap as he kissed me with renewed vigor.

So many emotions fluttered within me in that moment. I wanted to laugh, I wanted to cry, but mostly, I wanted to give into this mate bond and show him exactly how much he meant to me.

Something must've shot down the bond, because Callum abruptly broke away, glancing down to the way our bodies were tangled in each other as heat continued to blossom between us. "You're ready," he said in awe before meeting my gaze again. "And all it took was a near-death experience."

I lightly slapped him on the chest, a laugh tearing its way out of my throat. "I want *you*, Callum. More than I have ever wanted anything in my life, and perhaps the mate bond has a hand at speeding up the process, but…I'm okay with that."

Callum shook his head. "But here? Now? On the dirty attic floor?" he tsked. "That's so unlike you, Banana."

My heart nearly sung at the stupid nickname he had conned for me. "Doesn't matter," I said, shifting my position so I was straddling his hips. My most sensitive spot practically screamed at the pressure, at lightly scaping against his growing bulge. "I just want *you*."

Callum chuckled, pulling me closer to him. "Come here." And then, his lips were upon mine once again, traveling downward, nipping at my chin, the underside of my face, my neck—

"I never thought I'd see the day when I finally got to witness the mate bond in action," a high-pitched voice suddenly said from behind.

I froze, my hands still tangled in Callum's hair with his teeth just inches from my collarbone. And to my horror, the heat we had felt just moments before quickly retracted into itself, leaving a cold, vacant space where it once was.

Callum broke away from my neck, his expression showing he was equally horrified, before we scrambled to untangle ourselves to face our intruder head-on.

An intruder who just interrupted the most pivotal moment of my life. An intruder whose voice I absolutely did *not* recognize.

My heartrate skyrocketed as my gaze landed on what was perhaps one of the most beautiful women I had ever seen. Her skin was lightly sun-kissed, long, black hair streaking down her back and fanning at her hips. A knowing smirk lit up her features as she gazed at us curiously with deep green eyes.

Callum shifted his position, lightly pushing me so I was behind him. *Danger!* my mind yelled, but as to why the woman was dangerous, I didn't know.

Aside from the fact she broke into my parents' home and then snuck into the attic without Callum nor I hearing anything.

And then, Callum finally broke the silence, hostility radiating off him in waves. "What do you want, Sahara?"

Sahara? The name didn't ring any bells to me, but that didn't mean shit when Callum was practically staring daggers at her.

The witch I ran into in the woods that one day, Callum told me, once again reading my thoughts. *I'm almost positive that's her, though the skin she's wearing right now isn't her true form.*

What? My mind was spinning with this revelation, my human mind struggling to comprehend what he was saying. There was a witch *here* in my attic, one of the ones responsible for cursing my village. And judging by how she carried herself, something told me she knew we had broken the curse by killing off the werewolves.

Sahara took a step forward. "Relax. I'm not here to hurt your mate." She paused, her eyes finally landing on me, though why, I didn't know.

Yet, Callum said into my mind, causing my hackles to rise. "Then, why are you here?" he growled to the witch.

"For her," Sahara said bluntly. "There's strong witch blood in her, though I surmise it's less than twenty-five percent of her lineage."

It was as if the entire world froze, my mate and I hanging onto every word she said. This wasn't possible. It *couldn't* be possible. I was as human as they came; there was no way I was a witch as well.

Callum was the first to break the silence. "Impossible!" he snarled.

Sahara shrugged. "My senses don't lie, much like yours don't, wolf," she said. "In fact, if I had to guess, I would say she belongs to *us,* to *our* coven."

Strong alpha power suddenly shot down the mate bond, nearly knocking me over, as fur sprouted all over Callum's arms. "You can't have her," he snarled as his limbs jutted out, shredding through the thin clothing he was wearing, until he was on all fours, the same magnificent white wolf I came to know.

And that was when all hell broke loose.

EPILOGUE

CALLUM

All I saw was red. Pulsing, blinding red as rage infiltrated every pore of my skin, infecting my bones with its poison. All of it directed at the witch in front of me, someone who at one point had been an ally to my pack.

Not anymore, I grumbled in my mind, and my wolf had to agree. Because part witch or no, Savannah was *mine*, and I wouldn't let anyone take her from me.

If Sahara knew what was good for her, she would back away right now. After all, she wasn't stupid. She had to know how much of an uproar this would cause, considering our growing mate bond.

But the witch didn't bat an eyelash. "Stand down, wolf, if you know what's good for you. I have orders from Willow herself to bring the girl to us. As one of ours, she is under *our* jurisdiction and must answer for her crimes."

A howl ripped up my throat before I lunged at her, my mind made up. I almost lost her, and I wasn't in the business of losing her again. My claws outstretched as they sunk into her flesh, and Sahara let out a piercing shriek.

Her form flickered between her glamor and her real appearance before finally settling on her true form, long limbs snaking around my back and nails latching onto my flesh. Magic exploded out of her, and I was thrown back, my side making contact with the wall.

"Callum!" I heard Savannah scream as I fell, black spots dancing across my vision. I looked just in time to see her crawl towards me before Sahara threw another blast of magic at her, causing her to lie flat on her back.

Savannah coughed, vines snaking around her form to hold her in place as if she were nothing more than the witch's latest catch, nothing more than dirt.

Something broke in me then as I watched her struggle, as I watched the vines cocoon her in a makeshift prison, uncomfortably digging into her as she screamed. This was what Sahara had tried to warn me about that day in the woods. This was vengeance against us destroying the curse, and now, my mate was left to pay the price.

"I was going to do this the easy way, but you left me no

choice," Sahara said. "This is non-negotiable, wolf. The girl is ours, and therefore, it is entirely within our right to do what is best."

By caging her? My wolf was just as confused as I, and I shot that thought into her mind, my only way of communicating while in this form. *You said you weren't here to hurt her!*

Sahara shrugged. "Small technicality." She chuckled. "After all, you guys *did* destroy our curse after I explicitly warned you not to, and since she's one of ours, well...it only seemed fitting I take her back with me so she can answer to her crimes. You, on the other hand, I should just kill you where you stand, but if I did that, I'm sure I'd have to answer to your father. No, I figured taking your mate would be a more than suitable punishment, especially when you never learn of her fate."

No! I shot into her, forcing my limbs to cooperate. Sahara turned away from me, her eyes on the prize, as she stalked closer to Savannah.

I stood on wobbly legs, both sides of me finally in sync for the first time as we stared at our opponent. Sahara wanted a war, and she would get one.

Before I gave her the chance to catch whiff of what I was doing, I lunged, sinking my teeth into her neck and yanking as hard as I could. Sahara howled as her feet slid out from under her, her body thrown about as I shook her every which way to disorient her.

The taste of blood filled my mouth, and I chomped

harder until my teeth crunched bone. The witch stilled, and then, I severed her head from her body with one clean bite.

Several things happened at once.

Sahara's body dropped from my muzzle as her head rolled to the other side of the attic.

The vines started retracting from Savannah's form, since the witch who had caused them was now dead.

And Savannah was staring at me, horrified at my bloodied appearance, at what I just had to do.

Slowly, she pushed herself up on steady legs, her eyes traveling between me and the witch's head, her face screwed in concentration. And then, she returned her gaze to me once again.

And the first words out of her mouth were, "What the fuck just happened?"

ACKNOWLEDGEMENTS

I wrote the majority of this book during NaNoWriMo in 2022. Back then, Savannah and Callum had just been a concept, and though I knew the general direction of where this book was going to go, the rest had been up to figuring out along the way. This is my first book not associated with the World of Roseway universe, and this is also my first romance-heavy book. As such, here are the people I would like to thank the most.

To my family. Thank you for constantly believing in me and pushing me to be my best.

To my beta readers. Thank you for helping me make this book the best it can be.

To my friends, both near and far. Thank you for the constant support.

Lastly, to you, the reader. Thank you for giving this book a chance, and I hope you enjoy!

ABOUT THE AUTHOR

N. M. Lambert is a part-time writer, editor, avid reader and gamer, and a heavy metal enthusiast. She graduated from Northern Arizona University with a bachelor's in both criminology and anthropology and with minors in both French and psychology. When not writing, she can be seen surfing the web, singing and sometimes trying to perfect her metal growls, and spending way too much time on Animal Crossing, Oblivion, and Skyrim. She currently lives in Pollock Pines, California with her family and a menagerie of dogs, birds, and a cat.